Truth and Dare

by

Ann M. Trader

The Wonder of Wildflowers, Book One

Publishing History
First Edition, 2024
Trade Paperback ISBN 978-1-5092-5579-5
Digital ISBN 978-1-5092-5580-1

The Wonder of Wildflowers, Book One
Published in the United States of America

Praise

If Ever in Love

"A stunning romance from start to finish. I strongly recommend this book!"

~Nancy, N. N. Light's Book Heaven

"If Ever in Love is a lovely historical romance set just after the American Revolution. It's a story of second chances and forgiveness. Sometimes, the hardest to forgive is ourselves."

~Sherri Lupton Hollister, author and member of Heart of Carolina Romance Writers

"I particularly enjoyed Trader's style and how well-written the novel was throughout."

~Goodreads Review

Crinkles All the Way

"Crinkles All the Way has everything a reader could want in a holiday romance: a vibrant community, fun supporting characters, a swoony hero, a relatable heroine, and a touch of Christmas magic. "

~Melissa McTernan, author The Wild Rose Press

The Gingerbread Cookie Code

"The Gingerbread Cookie Code moves quickly, but it leaves nothing to the imagination and sends you on a steamy ride that is sure to capture your heart."

~D. M. Grant, author The Wild Rose Press and blogger.

Dedication

For wildflowers like Goldie, remember…you are enough.

Acknowledgements

I first began writing *Truth and Dare* as a short story for a romance anthology, but it quickly grew into something more. Much more. Goldie and Max's romance sparked the idea for a series, the Wonder of Wildflowers, and I can't wait to write all the stories of this amazing family!

I want to thank my writing group and beta readers for helping me improve my craft. This is my fourth book with The Wild Rose Press, and I appreciate their commitment to author growth and development. I'm especially grateful for Judi Mobley, my talented and thoughtful editor. And to my family, I love you!

Chapter One

Monday, May 10th 9:55 a.m.
Max
I flexed my hand, weaving the worn leather band between my fingers, wrapping it around my thumb twice. I tugged on it until my pulse thrummed at the tip of my finger, then released it. My dad scribbled on his tablet while I repeated the motion. He tapped the screen one last time, flipped the cover closed, and steepled his hands beneath his chin.

"Jesus, Max. I don't have to tell you we've got a lot riding on this. Hundreds of hours invested in this project." Dad scowled, eyes gimlet gray. "Ethan's out—that means you're in."

I stuffed the band into my pocket, grabbed the arms on my chair, and leaned forward. Dad hired Ethan right out of college seven years ago, had me train him, and made him our geotechnical engineering supervisor a few years back. That I couldn't remember the guy ever being out for sickness didn't matter. Sure, I could take his place. Hell, it might even be fun getting my hands dirty in the field again. I swore under my breath, completely pissed at the situation, then looked at my dad. "Why am I always the clean-up hitter around here?"

"That's a matter of perspective. I consider you my best closer."

My dad played shortstop on a college scholarship,

1

so my family batted baseball jargon around every day…only I wasn't in the batting mood.

Dad folded his arms over his chest, giving me a pithy glare. "Look, this is no one's fault. It's appendicitis, which means Ethan's having an emergency appendectomy. Today. The client is expecting top brass from Corda Design and Development tomorrow, and no one fits that description better than you."

"You do."

Dad lifted his eyebrows when he looked at me. "You'd better get packed."

"Look," I began, scrubbing my hands on my thighs, "normally I wouldn't care, and you know it. But I need to be in Charlotte this week. It's too damn far for me to drive back and forth each day."

The client was Shembery Isle, a quaint coastal town near Charleston, South Carolina and some two hundred fifty miles away from Charlotte.

"Which is why we've booked the resort on the south side of the island for the week."

I groaned. "I'm up to my eyeballs with the Santoro project, and there's Hazelton Municipal, Jensen Hydraulics—"

Dad cut me off with the snap of a binder clip around a stack of vouchers, his code for *case closed.*

I lowered my eyes and ran my finger over the monogram on the cuff of my shirtsleeve. Our company ran on a high speed network, used two-factor authentication and 5G wireless, and paid for the best engineering design and financial system software in the industry. Nothing required paper anymore, but at Dad's insistence, we still pushed around expense reports and purchase orders. Secretly, I was convinced he kept us stocked with bond paper and black binder clips just so he could flick them at us when the mood struck him.

I loved the guy, but that didn't stop me from casting him a look that'd shave a year off most men. But not my dad. *Balls of fucking steel.* I cracked my knuckles and pushed out a breath.

Dad leaned forward. "Look at you—you're as tight as a slingshot. The trip won't be all work, you know. Relax, enjoy the beach and some fresh seafood. A week away from the office will do you good."

My skin prickled beneath my starched collar, and I stood, sending my chair skidding backward. "Let me be clear. I've got things to do here. Send James."

His phone rang, and with a quick glance, he silenced it. "Son, you know with Annabel on bedrest, his place is here."

I weighed the truth of this statement, then sank back into the chair. I loved my younger brother. James was as true a gem as you'd ever find, the guy who buys drinks for everybody at the bar and never forgets your birthday. As if I needed reminding he was the picture of domesticity with his soulmate wife, a lakefront home just outside of Charlotte, and a baby on the way, I growled. I mean, I *literally* growled.

"Damn it, I've got Ashley's university tenure banquet Thursday night. I can't miss it. I-I gave her my word."

Dad pressed his hands into a single fist on his desktop, his lengthy sigh a signal he cared little for the muck I'd made of my marriage. "She's your ex-wife, Max. *Ex.* There's a statute of limitations on such promises, and hers ran out when the ink dried on the divorce papers."

As my fingers curled around the armrests, I released my own lengthy sigh and drew my eyebrows down. On a deeper level I hesitated to acknowledge, I knew my dad was right. Ashley and I were good and divorced, parted like a fork in a river. But as we'd stood in the lobby of our attorney's office four months ago, my escort to the tenure banquet had been her parting request. *It's the most important night of my life, Maxie. You'll still take me, won't you? Please…?*

In hindsight, I should've been pissed that our wedding day didn't qualify as her 'most important' anything. But the urgency in her tone paired with her limpid gaze had tugged on my heartstrings. And with my judgment clouded in a fog of lingering sentimentality, I'd agreed.

Hammer.

The vein in my forehead throbbed, an undeniable truth whooshing through my brain. All that remained from our nine-year marriage—outside of my alimony check, two ridiculously expensive sets of designer luggage, and a hand-scribbled custody agreement for MerryBelle, our Scottish Terrier—was this promise and the damn bracelet in my pocket.

Nail.

I blew out another breath, only this time my shoulders shuddered under an even greater realization. *Am I the family screwup now?* There was a time when my little brother had run in high gear, driving our parents batshit with his hot car and even hotter girlfriends. But when James discovered during his senior year at State he needed a semester of foreign language to graduate, in walked Annabel DeJonge. The university's tutoring center assigned the lovely, dedicated exchange student from Martinique to my brother…and he came skidding to a halt. *A life-crashing brake-check.*

I smirked at the irony before wiping my hand over my mouth. *It's official.* James was the proverbial bedrock of our family, and I was a hunk of crack-ridden limestone.

Coffin.

"Max."

I jerked my head in Dad's direction and groaned. With a swift push out of my chair, I walked to the minibar and poured a finger of scotch into a tumbler. I ignored the flicker of confusion in his expression and tossed the drink down, staring into the empty glass. The liquor burned my throat and fired my resolve. I pivoted, armed with my fastball, when the door swung open and in walked Bedrock.

"Hey, Max! I've been looking for you," James said, eyes bright, rubbing his hands together. "Everything's all set. The plane's gassed up. Sofia's emailing you the flight plan, hotel confirmation, meeting—"

Dad's lips disappeared into a thin line.

I laid my glass on the counter with a thud.

James' gaze flickered between the two of us. "Will one of you tell me what the hell's going on?"

Engaged in a mental tug-of-war, I wanted to drag my dad over the top of his desk…but I couldn't do it. Myles Corda was the head of our family, the CEO of our company, and my boss. What was that when compared to one last promise to your overreaching ex-wife? *Damn.*

"Nothing. I was just filling Max in on a few details about the Shembery Isle project." Dad straightened in his chair. "I can rest easy knowing you'll oversee the on-site plans and design schematics. I knew I could count on

5

you, Son."

I pressed the heel of my hand against the ache in my head. *The Squeeze Play. I'm screwed.* No point prolonging the inevitable. "Well, if you'll both excuse me, I've got things to take care of—a tar and feathering from Ashley to endure—if I'm flying out this afternoon."

With his hands clasped behind his back, James rocked back and forth on his heels, and I cut him a sideways look.

Dad rolled his chair backward and waved his index finger. "Oh, and just one more thing before you go."

His tone tripped the check-engine light in my brain, and I arched a quizzical brow. I felt like I was trapped in a freeway traffic jam, idling on fumes, not a gas station in sight.

Dad cleared his throat. "Goldie Vreeland will accompany you to Shembery Isle. Ethan speaks highly of her work with the municipality. The town manager tells me she's creative and cooperative. Besides, she's been on the project since she came on board and can help you sell the benefits of our sustainability designs."

Fuck me. I raked my dad over with my gaze. "Not in the field, she hasn't. She has no track record outside this building." I shot a beseeching look at my brother. "How long's she been with us? A month…?"

James flashed me a swarthy smile. "You're slipping, Max. Try four."

Dad smirked at our exchange from above the rim of his glasses, then shook his head and dove into a stack of expense vouchers.

James was the one slipping. *Try seventeen weeks, three days*—I dragged my hand across the back of my neck, head bowed to steal a glance at my wristwatch—

6

and a handful of hours. Christ, my stalker's memory made even *me* flinch.

Which is exactly why I can't go it alone for a week with Goldie Vreeland.

After living in a marriage that masqueraded as the tundra, and during the yearlong waiting period for the divorce, I hadn't rubbed against a woman in some time. I served on the boards of several charities, and while their galas frequently required a date, I chose companions from my professional, friends-only zone. Though I wasn't a complete oaf in the relationship department—and despite my counselor's urging to 'get into the dating world already'—my neck warmed with thoughts about sharing the same space *with her*. At Shembery Isle for a week…for business or pleasure, or something in between.

I double-downed on my efforts, ever the go-to closer. "I don't give a shit. She'll only get in my way. I can get everything I need from Ethan."

James had his hand on the door, one foot crossed over his ankle. "I'm afraid he's already under the knife." He narrowed his gaze, green eyes so much like my own challenging. "C'mon, Max, what gives? Why are you always such a dick with Goldie? Fact is, she knows what she's doing, and the town's administration values her input. She may need your finesse and credibility with the client." He paused, seeming to consider something. "But you'll need her to bring your ass up to speed with the actual work."

I glared at them for several long moments before yanking my tie loose from my collar. I didn't need any reminders from my brother. When it came to Goldie Vreeland, I did my homework. I'd pulled her resume within hours of meeting her, committing her impressive credentials to memory. I remembered thanking God I didn't hire and supervise entry-level engineers anymore because my thoughts about her were in no way work-related.

Which again, is exactly why I can't go it alone for a week with Goldie Vreeland.

My scowl deepened, recollecting how the phrase 'dick with Goldie' fired my pulse while another sentence rambling around my brain thoroughly doused it. *When I ditch Ashley at her ever-loving tenure celebration, she'll kick my ass to Sunday.*

I grabbed my coat and slung it over my shoulder. "Fine. I'll take another one for the team." I made no effort to mask my ire. "Babysit the new girl. Close the damn deal."

James shook his head, chuckling under his breath.

Dad cocked his head, ballpoint pen poised in his hand, and eased into a smile. Our gazes met, as they always had, with hard-won respect. "Let me know when you land, Son. And thank you. I appreciate your commitment to the company...and me."

As I walked toward James, a smile crept across his face. "Safe trip, Big Brother. Try to enjoy yourself...at least a little." He leaned in, whispering conspiratorially. "I can think of worse things than 'babysitting' the lovely Ms. Vreeland on one of South Carolina's most beautiful islands."

I could think of worse things, too, but none of them changed the fact I felt cornered. *By responsibility and family, and as yet, my closely guarded attraction to Goldie.* As I elbowed past my brother, I flipped him the finger and strode down the hallway, fidgeting once again with the leather bracelet in my pocket.

Chapter Two

Goldie

To say Max Corda possessed a look of single-mindedness as he cut the corner from his father's office would be like saying a hummingbird merely flaps its wings. In the time I'd worked for Corda Design and Development—or CDD, for short—a privately owned engineering and planning corporation in Charlotte, I'd never seen Max so intense, so...*unnerved.* I'd never seen his father, brother—or anyone else at the company, for that matter—even the slightest bit intensely unnerved either. Unlike my capstone college internship with a state environmental agency that ran on cheap coffee and poorly disguised *good ole boy* doctrine, CDD fostered a respectful community of interdepartmental teams, all dedicated to providing impeccable client services.

Aside from the fact that CDD had been nothing short of a Godsend for my career, I'd found working in the same space as Max Corda professionally thrilling...and more than a little intimidating. From our initial introduction, with him seated beside his father at the conference room table, I'd fancied Max a DEFCON One—a serious nuclear threat to womankind. *Or at least to* this *woman.* Since then, every time I'd come within five feet of him, the combination of his affable grin and wide shoulders—housed in a six-foot three frame of

10

heart-stopping masculinity—sent sparks tingling through my body.

Max's eyes usually shone a green, somewhere between mossy fern and pine, but as he'd approached the elevator, they simmered like a pair of emeralds. He tapped his right foot and jabbed his finger on the call button. The line of his profile was chiseled, the ends of his black hair brushing his collar, a scowl bracketing his mouth.

I pretended indifference, ducking into the break room. *What a joke.* I was about as far away from indifference with Max Corda as my fingernail was to the knuckle on my pinky finger. Every quirk of his smile and glimmer of white teeth drew my attention like a heat-seeking missile.

I casually dropped my pen beside my foot and, bending to retrieve it, gazed at him from beneath my lashes. Sofia popped up beside him, tapping her fingers on her phone screen, then smiled when he gave her a flick of his head. And as if on cue, one perfect dark curl fell over his forehead right before he disappeared inside the elevator.

As Sofia approached, I straightened and leaned into the doorjamb. She was Max's personal assistant and the best friend I'd made since moving to Charlotte. I met her frowning face with a puzzled look of my own. "What's going on? I've never seen Max so pissed."

Sofia heaved an almost reverent sigh. "He hates conflict between his personal and professional life. It's been a rough year for him. So many loose ends." She scratched her jaw with the edge of her phone. "Max likes painting the canvas the way he sees it, not connecting someone else's random dots."

My shoulders softened, and our gazes met. Sofia had the shape of a hefty-sized hourglass and a propensity for colorful language. Married to one of Max's oldest friends, Sofia cast her net long and wide when it came to protecting her boss. Metaphor notwithstanding, I imagined anything bearing the mark of Max Corda could be deemed nothing less than a masterpiece.

Sofia motioned me into the break room and pulled a box of strawberry-iced breakfast tarts from the cabinet. She raised a questioning eyebrow.

"Do you even know the number of dyes in those things?" I masked a shudder behind a smile. "You know I like coloring in my crayons, not my food."

"Suit yourself, Goldenrod," she said, sinking her teeth into the pastry before continuing. "Max is a solid, straight-arrow kind of guy. He sees the white space, knows the best colors to use, and paints the thing fucking flawless." One corner of her mouth turned down. "If I could yank his ex-wife up by her toenails and drip hot wax on her cheeks, I would. The bitch still has him scattered all over the place, chasing dots."

I'd heard whispers around the office about Max's divorce. Ethan, who'd worked at the firm for seven years, described Ashley Windrow-Corda as a brilliant professor of economics. He claimed she came from old money, but her wit and style were far from stuffy. His statement had awakened the former beauty pageant competitor inside me, so I did what came naturally…and scoped her out on social media.

Yeah, bad idea.

As I'd scrolled through Ashley's photos and stories, my shoulders stiffened. The petite brunette looked stunning at the Women's League Holiday Fashion Show in a fitted embroidered dress, ruby red pumps, and a matching clutch. At her department's Casino Night fundraiser, she beat the house dressed in a sexy pantsuit at the blackjack table.

And the rest of the pictures—you know, the ones *without* her in them—highlighted her love of fine wine and old-world rustic homes. No offense to the charities themselves, but her posts advocating for juvenile diabetes and Parkinson's research were bitter pills, especially since she'd already won the lottery in brains and beauty. I wanted—no, I *needed*—her to be an emotionally vacuous soul.

I bit my lower lip, fighting a wave of inferiority. "Is she really that bad? D'you think he still has feelings for her?"

Sofia shook her head. "Nah, they were separated for a year before the divorce became final in January. As perfect as things looked on the outside, their relationship sucked. Tense, you know?" I nodded, and she tilted her head to one side. "Things seem to be getting better for him now it's officially over, but Ashley likes to keep one claw in him...and he's too damn patient with her."

I wedged my pen between my teeth, picturing his ex-wife like some sea serpent with her tentacles strangling him. "God, that's so messed up."

"Yeah, and I've watched her manipulate him for years." Sofia leaned in closer. "He shouldn't feel obligated to escort her to some fancy party either—some uptight *tenure* banquet at the university." She pulled back, crossing her arms. "Even though appendicitis must hurt like hell—and I hate it for sweet Ethan—at least Max can get out of the evening with a legit reason."

Lost in wayward thoughts about how a woman

who'd actually *had* Max Corda could've ever let him go, I nearly missed Sofia's comment. I turned, shaking my head. "Wait, what…?"

"Max. He's going with you, silly. To Shembery Isle. Duh…" She smiled, head seesawing while she dragged out the last syllable.

"What are you talking about?" I passed an uneasy hand across my collarbone. As recognition flared in my friend's dark eyes, her grin fell away.

Sofia sucked in a breath around the strawberry sprinkles stuck in the corner of her mouth. "Holy crap, you—you mean you don't know…?"

I hated this feeling. *You know the one that bounces around between ignorance and embarrassment, then leaves a sailor's knot in your throat?* I shook my head again.

"Ethan got sick last night. He's having an emergency appendectomy—like right now. He's going to be fine and all, but Mr. Corda is sending Max in his place this afternoon." As dawning flooded my face, Sofia squealed under her breath. "Oh my God, I mean, I thought you knew. Here, let me text you the details. Girl, I'm so excited for you!"

After thumbing her phone screen, Sofia grabbed my hand and led me into my office. I collapsed into my chair, my response turning from disbelief to dread—first for Ethan's health, then for my readiness to meet the client without him…but *with* Max Corda.

My mind sprinted through the hours of research underlying our sustainable design solutions and the presentation I'd finished just days ago. When I did the mock-rehearsal for Ethan, he liked how I identified the takeaway from the get-go—the nugget we wanted

Shembery's Board to keep circling back to—and supported our decisions with a tight structure of data. He'd called my angle inspired, but I dubbed it simple reverse psychology, explaining that was how I'd flourished in a family of eight.

As Sofia wiggled onto the corner of my desk, I pulled my lint roller out of the side drawer. I gripped it in my sweaty palm, running the adhesive down my arm, wishing my emotions were as easy to control as fluffs of lint. She ticked through the timeline of the past twelve hours down to the smallest detail—even the part where Max would be flying us in a private plane to the coast. If that wasn't enough to stop my stroke midway down the front of my slacks, her question certainly was.

I jerked forward. "What d'you mean, 'You got any condoms?' "

"You know. For safe sex," she shot back. "Max might not bring any, so make sure you have some. Just in case…you know…"

"Sofia!" I coughed a mortified sound over her name, my gaze swinging toward the mail courier as he shuffled past my office door. I lowered my voice. "Oh my God, whatever you're thinking is going to happen on this trip, it won't be a hookup."

Sofia crossed her arms and gazed at me from over her petal pink tortoise glasses. "Don't shit me. Are you telling me you haven't thought about it?"

My teeth dug into my bottom lip. I'd thought about it—and little else—for months.

"You've seen his perfect Roman nose, haven't you?" Sofia slid her index finger down the ridge of her nose in a sweeping motion.

I hastened a nod.

"Ever noticed how sturdy and long his fingers are…?"

I squeezed my eyes shut, her reference to what I imagined was a penis even Adonis would find impressive sending unruly sensations through my body. I cautiously opened one eye, then the other, a grin ghosting my lips.

"Uh-huh. You know I know you've thought about it." Sofia winked. "There's no need to be embarrassed because he's very fine and *very* single. And look at you, with a name like Goldenrod? It's like God showered you with sunshine, inside and out."

I stood and sidled up to her, flicking her arm with the lint roller. "Oh, stop it already. Can I help my mom was an English teacher and my dad was a farmer? They decided to blend the two things they loved most and gave us all wildflower names."

"I've seen the pictures of your brothers and sisters spread all over your apartment, Goldie. There's not a weed in the bunch."

I mulled over the image for a moment. Though my siblings and I were uncommonly close, we'd needed room to grow. My oldest brother, Ace, ran the family farm in Vista Falls, North Carolina, and he was a master at blending agricultural innovation with old-fashioned grit. My next brother, Thorne, was a former attorney in Georgia. Now he used his undergraduate degree in architectural history as an instructor at a private college and a historic preservation consultant. Youngest brother, Sage, pulled up his roots, following his dream across the country to be a screenwriter. My two sisters stayed in North Carolina like me, Primrose saving lives as a nurse in Raleigh and Billie shaping them as a middle school math teacher in our hometown. The Vreeland Wildflowers stood out in any crowd…and never wilted in the sun.

I swallowed hard and leaned in, squeezing her shoulder. "You're too much, you know that?"

Sofia smiled, touching the side of her head to mine and fanning her free hand like a panoramic camera. "Just imagine it—you and Max taking walks on the beach after long days at work…a couple bottles of wine with late-night suppers…" Her singsong tone drifted through the air.

As much as I wanted to be his co-star in that show, I had to be real. "But he doesn't even know I exist."

She turned to face me. "Oh no, let's get something straight. If there's one person I know, it's my boss. And nothing—and no one—gets past him. Trust me. Max knows who you are." She pushed off my desk and swung around, flashing me a teasing smile. "And perhaps he'll know you a little better after this trip." Her gaze shot over to my suitcase by the door, then back to me. "And you won't forget to bring some—"

"Yeah, yeah, I've got it. Even though I won't be needing them, I'll stop by the drugstore anyway. You know my obsessive nature won't let it go."

Sofia laughed, wagging her finger at me as she crossed the room. "Have a good time and text me, okay? I. Want. Details."

I gave her a smile, then after she sashayed out the door, I tucked it away.

And the irony of the situation hit home.

Me and Max Corda…in close proximity for the next ninety-six hours…engaged in a comprehensive exploration and assessment of natural passive management techniques for Shembery Isle's stormwater infrastructure system.

I closed my eyes and lifted my face toward heaven in silent prayer. *Oh yeah, and condoms...just in case.*

Chapter Three

Monday, May 10th 3:10 p.m.
Max

I stood on the tarmac at the municipal airport with the breeze at my back, pressed send on a text, and released a beleaguered groan. I steeled my resolve for the tongue lashing to come whenever I next spoke to Ashley. She'd curse me yet again as an unreliable, work-obsessed Neanderthal. *That's the pot calling the kettle black.* Or perhaps she'd call me an emotional misfit again. I bristled. *No amount of time will ever heal that cut.* I slid my phone into the hip pocket of my jeans and shoved the sound of her voice to the farthest corner of my mind.

I gazed at my wristwatch, then blinked at the sun, replaying the flight plan from memory. I zipped open my backpack, double-checking the essentials I'd flown with most of my life—bottled water, spearmint gum, acetaminophen, an apple, a can of roasted almonds, a box of malted milk balls…and my Swiss army knife. I slung the bag into the cockpit and chucked my suitcase inside the luggage compartment of the company's single engine passenger plane.

As I slid my sunglasses up the bridge of my nose, I glimpsed a minivan approaching in the distance. I turned my neck in a circle and cracked my knuckles to take the edge off my nerves.

What no one suspected—and only my counselor knew—was Goldie Vreeland had blipped my sensory radar on the daily since she joined the firm. The first signal registered the morning she walked into the conference room displaying a landscape of lithe legs and slender feet in leather pumps. When the sound of her laughter reached my ears, the signal quickly amped into a series of short, compressed chirping pulses. I considered this feat remarkable given my radar had been blip-free for much of the past decade. But any man with blood flowing through his veins had to have appreciated how the herringbone fabric of her pencil skirt hugged her curves, and the drape of her silk blouse enhanced her breasts.

Under the soft white track lighting in the conference room, her hair glistening like honeyed molasses, she'd slid into the seat Ethan held for her. When she turned her body toward him, swapping whispers and smiles behind the shield of his tablet, blood thrummed between my ears. With even breaths, I tempered my unexpected territorial reaction with images of Ethan, his lovely wife, and their three-year-old daughter. They were a warm and snug kind of family, caring and generous. Ethan gave Goldie the same smile he gave everyone. *Genuine.* With my testosterone back in check, I'd taken my seat beside Dad, gazed at the line of engineers and statisticians assembled around the rectangular table, and relaxed into a half-smile.

The minivan came to a halt, pulling me out of my head. I overheard Goldie thanking the driver, and when she stepped out—the miles of her exposed legs reaching the ground—I was grateful my sunglasses concealed my appreciative gaze. I cocked my head, calculating her height when she stopped several feet in front of me. While she was tall, I was certain with her wrapped inside my arms, her head would fit like a puzzle piece beneath my chin.

"Hi, Mr. Corda!" Goldie waved a greeting, the sun's rays kissing her cheeks, her smile wrecking my concentration like a demolition ball. She wore a fitted blue jean jacket over a brick red dress that skimmed her knees, long hair falling in billowy waves over her shoulders. She removed her sunglasses and hooked the arm over her neckline, smack down the middle of her cleavage.

I swallowed hard and closed the space between us in two steps. "Hello, Goldie. Nice to see you." I took charge of her two bags and inclined my head toward the plane. "You know, I can't allow you in the cockpit unless you agree to call me Max. My dad is Mr. Corda."

She lifted her face into the breeze and slid her hands inside her jacket pockets. "I wasn't sure—I mean, I didn't want to presume."

My gaze followed her tongue as it darted out of her mouth, licking her lips, and damn if that swipe didn't sock me right in the gut.

Waiting, she raised her delicate eyebrows.

I checked my errant thoughts, sighing. "Yes, of course, and that's fair. Actually, I appreciate the show of respect. It's kind of rare these days with people your—"

Age, a small voice filled in. I lowered my head, dragging my hand across my neck. Christ, I could have written my stupid thought in the sky with less fanfare than this.

As I pulled my gaze up to her face, her mouth curved at the corners in a sort of easy fondness. The warmth of her smile had me reeling on the inside.

And then she blinked, and the look was gone. "I don't think you'll find me like most twenty-four-year-olds."

I cleared my throat, needing to untangle my mess. "May I start over, please?"

She nodded.

"I'm not your boss, and it'd make me happy if you called me Max. I want this week to be comfortable for both of us." I smiled, and she allowed a small one back at me. "I've heard good things about you, Goldie. I look forward to getting to know you better."

She pulled her lip into her mouth then full-on grinned. "That's good because I feel the exact same way. Thank you, Max."

Grateful, I stashed her luggage in the hull, locked the door, and turned toward her. "Tell me, have you flown much?"

"Nothing like this." Goldie raised her hand to shield the sun from her eyes. "Until a few hours ago, I thought it'd be Ethan and me in a company car." Her gaze traveled from the nose to the tail of the plane, then back to me. "It must slap to be a pilot."

I blinked a few times to keep from rolling my eyes. *Thirty-one never felt so damn old.* And for the second time in as many minutes, I was wondering if I should have my hands gripped on the control wheel of this plane or wrapped around a glass of Metamucil. *And this is the reason my little sister calls me* cheugy.

I turned back to her. "Yeah. Yeah, I suppose it does. *Slap.*"

She sucked in a squeaky breath, raising the heel of her hand to her temple. "Oh God, I'm such a ditz. I'm sorry. I just meant how cool—"

I shook my head, chuckling. "Hey, it's okay, Goldie. Really. I get it." My slang—like many things in my life—needed an overhaul. *You could help me with this. I'm a fast learner.*

I led her to the passenger door and helped her into the seat, resisting the urge to lean forward. While I needed to demonstrate how to fasten the seat belt and shoulder harness around her body, I couldn't risk veering too close to *them.* So, I did my best imitation of a flight attendant, gesturing through the motions in the air. I felt her gaze on my hands, and the warmth of it made my fingers twitch.

"So." I took a step backward. "Why don't you give it a go?"

I gripped the doorframe and watched her steady hands snap the series of buckles in place, smoothing the belts over her breasts. Much like the seven times I'd been stuck with her in the small space of the elevator at work, her scent of vanilla and honeysuckle reached my nose. I pulled my gaze up to her face as she tugged on the straps.

She turned her head toward me. "Whoa, what is it?" she asked, looking up and down her body.

If you only knew.

I should've told her to stop trying to puzzle me out because her bright bluebell eyes would never see what I saw. The 'it' was more than her lovely neck and blushed cheeks, though I had to admit they monopolized my thoughts whenever she huddled around Sofia's desk at lunchtime.

No, she'd never guess the 'it' came from little things, like watching her share her umbrella with our receptionist during an afternoon rain shower…and spotting a skein of yarn and sewing needles stuffed in the outside pocket of her leather satchel. *Damn, it must slap to be wrapped up in something you've knitted.*

"Are they too loose?" Goldie asked, tugging harder on the straps. "Like not safe for flying?"

Her question pulled me back to the present, and I mustered a grin, stuffing my hands in my jeans pockets. "Not a chance. You did great."

Her mouth curved into a cute little bow, and I waited several silent beats before closing her door, walking around the plane, and climbing into my seat.

I started the engine, the vibrations traveling through my feet and up my calves. As the plane came to life, so did my senses. Shifting air drafts whirred around us, the soft creaks in the frame reminding me of a house settling. While awaiting instructions from air traffic control, I glanced over at Goldie, her bottom lip wedged between her teeth, hands in a knot on her lap. *Holy shit.* As a big brother not only to James, but my twenty-two-year-old sister, Jess, giving a calming touch was part of my DNA. Though my feelings for Goldie were miles away from brotherly, the instinct to comfort was the same.

I placed my hand on the back of her headrest and waited until I had her gaze. "Hey. Don't worry, okay? I've logged hundreds of hours as a pilot. I've got this. Promise."

Goldie whooshed out a breath, then dropped her gaze and whispered, "Thank you."

Wanting to help her feel more at ease, I reached for my backpack, digging around inside. "Would you like something to drink or a snack? I've got an apple, some roasted almonds...a carton of malted milk balls?"

"Actually, I brought my own. But thanks anyway."

She folded her arms over her satchel, softly biting her bottom lip.

Damn, she's cute. Curious, I craned my neck in her direction. "So, what'd you bring? Maybe we could trade or something." As she poked around in her bag like a squirrel foraging for acorns, my smile grew.

"Um, I got a couple bags of pistachios, a peach, some carrot sticks," she said, tilting her head and finally looking up at me. "And a pack of cinnamon rice cakes."

I faltered for a moment. *Jesus, your eyes are as clear as the sky ahead of us.* Something in the way they twinkled appealed to my baser instincts. I was an accomplished engineer and a business professional. *Am I or am I not* The Closer? With Goldie, I wanted to be a man who acted on impulse. I wanted to flirt and unsettle her…just a little.

"I like peaches. Tell you what," I said, rubbing my knuckles over my lip. "Why don't we trade—my apple for your peach."

I held on to my breath while she pulled an adorable face and relaxed when the corners of her mouth curled up.

"Deal." Goldie smiled and dropped the peach in my palm, and I gave her my apple. She cupped it in her hands, peeking up at me from beneath those sweeping eyelashes. "You know, this is the most exciting thing I've ever done. Flying must be your favorite thing to do, huh?"

I leaned in her direction, close enough to catch the scent lifting off her sunshine-soft hair. I paused, all too aware hasty responses made for slippery slopes, and with one wrong word I might land on my ass.

When at last she met my gaze, I shrugged one

shoulder and with barely a hitch in my voice, said, "Almost."

Her chin dropped for several long seconds, then she closed her mouth, shaking her pretty head to hide the smile pinking her cheeks.

That right there felt good. *Damn good.*

As the voice of air traffic control broke the silence, I bit back a grin of my own and handed her a set of noise reduction headphones. I slid my sunglasses into place, put on my headset, and turned my attention to the runway. *Slap.*

Chapter Four

Monday, May 10th 4:40 p.m.
Goldie
I was right.
What.
A.
High.
Even with his backpack strapped in place, my carry-on rolling behind him, and two bags slung over his shoulder, Max still managed to catch my elbow when my knees wobbled on our way to the terminal. His scent of sandalwood and leather filled the space between us, a heady mix given my sensory overload from the spectacular flight.

Max secured our rental SUV, then drove us onto the highway toward Shembery Isle. Some twenty minutes later, we cruised along a coastal boulevard, windows lowered as he meandered the quieter streets. With my sunglasses on, I breathed in the sea salt air, soaking up the ambiance of the beach town. Strands of Spanish moss hung from live oak trees, and palmettos blew lazily with the wind. Spacious wood homes in hues of peach and lemon stood amongst a landscape of wildflowers, seagrass, and driftwood.

We soon arrived at the resort, and after checking in at the front desk—with Max clocking a half-dozen steps behind me—we crossed the lobby to the elevator. When his phone pinged, he pulled it from his pocket. I fixed my gaze on the swirls in the marble floors, attempting to appear disinterested. As he chuckled, I lifted my head, and he cracked a small smile. Moments later, he held the elevator door for me then pressed his finger on the illuminated button number three, quirking an eyebrow in my direction.

I nodded. "Same."

Before I could process the butterfly cyclone swirling in my belly—which had nothing to do with the lift and everything to do with how Max upended my nerves—I scooted out the moment the doors opened.

"Hey, Goldie?"

I pivoted, flashing Max my signature pageant smile—my go-to response for all anxiety-ridden situations.

He walked toward me, thumb hooked under the shoulder strap of his bag, and smiled. *Clearly, he aces the masculinity test with no preparation at all.* He tilted his head, like he was thinking over something. Obviously, he had no idea he could ask me anything, and I'd say yes. Readily. *Breathlessly.*

"So," he said, dragging out the word, "about dinner tonight—"

"Oh, I got it," I said, waking up my phone. "Sofia texted me everything. Reservations downstairs at seven o'clock." From the look of his furrowed brow, I wondered if I had a fleck of apple skin stuck between my teeth from my mid-flight snack.

"Yeah…there's been a slight change of plans. You and Ethan were having dinner downstairs. I have something else planned for us."

Us. The word sounded dreamy coming from his

mouth, floating through the air like a kite in springtime. My toes curled inside my sandals.

"That text," he said, gaze flickering to his phone, "was from one of my best friends from college. We're meeting him and his wife for supper. I don't know what the hell got into Ethan." He rubbed his knuckles under his chin. "You can't come to the coast and eat hotel food. Even *this* hotel's food."

I tucked a strand of hair behind my ear. "No, of course not."

"We're meeting Jack and Leigh at Thibodeaux's at eight."

Thibodeaux's. The name twirled through my thoughts.

Max leaned a shoulder on the wall, and our gazes met. "It's this fantastic urban grill—gorgeous waterfront views—fresh catch served daily. Exceptional food and service—"

As exceptional as you…?

"—so, how's that sound?"

My heart skipped a pair of beats, then I relaxed into my natural Goldie grin. "Sounds wonderful."

The corners of his mouth turned up. "Great. I'll come by at seven, room—" he said, cutting his gaze to my key card, "three eighteen."

I bobbed my head. "Seven o'clock. I'll be ready. And thank you, Max."

"My pleasure."

I waited, fidgeting with my card as Max strolled down the hallway, passing one…two…three doors. Three had been my lucky number ever since my dad read to me, what he affectionately renamed, *Goldenrod and the Three Bears.* Good things came in threes: bears, musketeers, little pigs, amigos, the buttons on the trumpet I played in the high school band. *And our rooms on the third floor.*

I turned and unlocked the door, stepping inside a suite awash in orange rays from the late day sun. I tossed my bags on the loveseat and strolled into the bedroom, flopping on the mattress and squealing a cry of delight into the bed pillows.

After a hot shower, slathering a honey oat body butter over every inch of my skin, I checked my reflection in the floor-to-ceiling bedroom mirror. The knee length sheath dress caressed my hips and legs. Its simple elegance embodied one of my mother's cornerstone beliefs—nothing beats the little black dress.

A trio of knocks interrupted my thoughts, and I glanced at my watch. *Right on time.* My shoes—timeless black Italian leather pumps worth every dollar I doled out on them—clicked on the parquet tile as I approached the door...and opened it to *him.*

Max's muscular frame filled the doorway, a mesmerizing vision, sexy as hell and completely effortless on his part. He had the lean, sculpted torso and long legs of a runway model, but none of the cushy edges. I leaned on the door, imagining his physique was every tailored suit's dream. *Every woman's, too.* I swallowed a tiny sigh, convinced God must've cashed in all His chips when He created Max Corda.

I straightened, holding my purse in my hands. "Hi."

"Hello," Max said, smiling.

I caught myself gazing at his lips a little too long, and looked away, praying I wasn't wearing a blush to match my heated cheeks.

"You look lovely." He crossed his arms, the move

accentuating the breadth of his chest. "I know we're here on business." His gaze skimmed up and down my body. "But when you come to the door looking like this, Shembery's integrated water management strategies are the last thing on my mind."

My breath hitched, awestruck his thoughts mirrored mine. I'd studied Max to distraction for seventeen weeks, four days—no, make that three—and I liked him. *Very much.*

I met his gaze, my fingers squeezing my kidskin leather clutch. If not for my experience holding a pose under stage lights and a judge's scrutiny, I might have toppled over at his appraisal. I couldn't decide what baffled me more: my being with Max Corda...or him seeming happy to be with me.

I tilted my head, wondering if the thrill of him would ever wear off. Somehow I doubted it would, so I decided to take a chance and run with it. "Sorry if I've distracted you."

I watched him lock the door behind us, and after signaling with an open palm for me to lead the way, he relaxed his hands at his sides. I peeked at his long index finger when he pressed the elevator call button, imagining it knew exactly where to roam on a woman's body.

"Feel free to distract me anytime, Peach."

Peach...?

Oh.

My.

God.

****

Max

We arrived at Thibodeaux's with time to spare, and

31

the host led us into the dining room. With Goldie by my side, I sensed the air in the room shift...and for good reason. She glided across the floor, shoulders straight, amber hair cascading down her back. The bodice of her dress wasn't revealing, baring nothing of her front or back, but it framed her breasts perfectly. Her leather pumps showcased her tight calves and tush, and both made my pulse hum.

I spotted Jack from across the room, his arm resting over Leigh's shoulder as he spoke into her ear. Her lips curled into a bashful yet intimate smile, and I found myself hoping I could illicit that kind of response in Goldie someday. A week ago, I was plowing through my backlog at work and questioning my sanity for agreeing to escort Ashley to her tenure banquet. And now I was on a week-long business trip to a beautiful island, out for the evening with two of my best friends...and one very sweet and lovely Peach. My mouth twitched. *I could get used to this.*

I held Goldie's chair, and she cast me an appreciative smile before I slid into the chair beside her. After introducing her to my friends, the server came to take our orders and returned with a bottle of Chardonnay minutes later.

Jack smiled, filled our glasses, and raised his own. "Here's to old friends...and new beginnings."

We drank to his toast and slid into easy conversation. Jack and I were fellow engineers and rowers in college, and he met Leigh at his cousin's wedding the summer after graduation. They were both members of the wedding party and pretty much inseparable after that weekend. They got married the following year and started their family right away. They were nothing like Ashley and me. *At all.*

Jack turned to Goldie. "I have to say I was a little surprised to hear from Max today. He's been holed up in Charlotte for so long I thought he must have lost his pilot's license. So," he said, grinning and crossing his arms on the table, "how'd you manage to get this guy out of the office and to the beach for work?"

Her knee brushed against mine as she shifted in her seat, and I watched—*enthralled*—as she smiled over the rim of her glass. "Oh, it wasn't me. We have *Mr.* Corda to thank for that."

When Jack arched a brow, I shrugged. "Ethan got appendicitis and needed emergency surgery. James is on lockdown with Annabel's baby-watch. You know the client always comes first with Dad, so he called me up." I took a sip of wine and turned toward Goldie, my lips forming a smile. "And I have to say I'm not complaining."

Jack scratched his chin. "Myles Corda isn't stupid. When the game's on the line, he knows you're his best pinch hitter."

I chuckled behind my hand. "He actually called me his best closer."

"Best closer?" Jack grinned, leaning forward on his elbows. "How about best—"

"Guys," Leigh said, smiling and waving her glass like a flag of surrender. "While this is enormously entertaining for Goldie and me, maybe you two could tone it down just a *teensy* bit?"

Jack reached over and kissed Leigh's knuckles, and I turned to Goldie, meeting her inquisitive gaze. "Sorry we get carried away sometimes. It's a baseball thing. I'll explain later."

"Promise…?" she asked, a hint of flirtation in her voice.

The air between us simmered, and as I cocked my head, enjoying the way the candlelight flickered over her cheek, I flexed my hand to keep from dragging my thumb across her smooth skin. I couldn't help but smile and reply with a heartfelt, "Absolutely."

As Jack changed the subject on his next breath, describing his latest fishing excursion on the Intercoastal Waterway, I gazed at the two women, their shoulders touching as Leigh swiped through the gallery of photographs on her phone. Still fit and trim, you'd never guess by looking at Leigh she was the mother of three incredible children.

Our server brought our entrees. Goldie dined on sea island shrimp and grits, and I enjoyed the blackened mahi and blue crab. After savoring both the wine and conversation, we ordered dessert, and when the ladies excused themselves to the powder room, Jack kicked my foot under the table.

"What the actual fuck, Corda? There's no way in hell this is a business trip. Not with the vibe you two have going on," he said, wagging his finger between me and Goldie's empty seat.

My smile was a faint tilt of my mouth. "Technically, it's business."

"Well, from where I'm sitting, *non-technically*, it looks like some damn good foreplay."

I turned to Jack, one elbow on the table. "I hardly know what that is anymore. Ashley conditioned me to weekly Saturday night sex."

He smirked over the rim of his glass. "Leaving you to service yourself the other six days, I guess?"

I chuckled at his keen summation, swirling the wine around in my glass and trying not to appear too pathetic. I took a last swallow and lowered my glass. "Well, the divorce is finally behind me, and I want to move on."

"I hope to hell you do, preferably with Goldie. She's perfect for you. I like her, Leigh likes her." My attention darted his way, and Jack raised his chin, smiling. "Oh, yeah. Leigh already gave me the look. When she grins at me and toys with her *second* earring, she's signaling full steam ahead."

Since my experience with unspoken marital language was the passive-aggressive type, I couldn't relate.

Jack topped off our glasses. "Look, Max. You're the most standup guy I know. You always put everyone's needs before your own. It's what you do." He pointed his drink at me. "But you need to listen to me on this, 'cause I know what you're thinking. I'm telling you, you're not a failure. You had a marriage, and in my humble opinion, it failed because you and Ashley were never in love."

My gaze narrowed.

"You weren't. Not really. You know it, and I know it. She was your first serious relationship, and she came in this lovely, perfect little package. Looks, brains, pedigree…" Jack paused for a sip before continuing. "When you married her right out of college, hell I didn't know anything about love. If I had, I'd have at least tried to stop you—might could've spared you the past decade in relationship hell."

I tapped my finger on my glass. I'd unpacked a lot of shit in counseling over the past year, but Jack hit on something we might have missed. *Failure.* The sense if I'd only listened better or paid closer attention to Ashley, we might have lasted. I drew down my brows, wondering if I'd agreed to take her to this tenure banquet out of some misplaced guilt about failing her.

I hated losing, and Jack understood that. I cut him a sideways glance. "Maybe you're right. When I moved out, I did feel like I'd come in second place." I pushed out a slow breath. "Less-than-my-best, you know?"

He nodded. "It tanked because neither of you were in love…not because you failed."

Damn. The idea intrigued me, and I was busy dissecting it when our server placed dishes of tiramisu on the table.

"So, with that cleared up, thank you very much," Jack said, flicking his head toward his wife and Goldie, "you've got about ten seconds to get your shit together and move on with your life. With Goldie."

I scratched my chin. "Leigh's really rubbed off on you."

"Can't be married to a couple's counselor for seven years and not learn a few things," he said out the corner of his mouth, smiling as we rose to greet the ladies.

I held the chair for Goldie, my gaze drifting from the exquisite column of her neck to her dazzling smile, complete with freshly glossed lips. I considered their fine form and shape, but almost more importantly, how perfectly they matched her brilliant mind. I took my seat beside her, and she gazed at me like I was anything but a misfit.

As Jack launched into the story about the flat tire our bus had on the way to a rowing competition in Alabama, I rested my arm on the back of Goldie's chair. As if it had a mind of its own, my hand found its way to the cloud of hair covering her back. I rubbed a few strands between my fingers, and she peeked at me from over her shoulder, the whiff of a smile on her lips. She turned back around, tilting her head in concentration on Jack's story, and when she offered a witty comeback, we all laughed.

I raised my glass to my lips, drinking in the wine...and Goldie. My thoughts hopscotched through the months I'd spent observing her. Whether addressing an advisory board on civic infrastructure investment, consulting with a subcontractor on optimum soil drainage protocols...or swapping stories with Sofia when they thought I was out of earshot, her mind fascinated me. It forced me to sit up, take notice, and want to be on my best behavior.

Or, if tonight's any indication, dare me to misbehave...

The notion rocked me, urging me to explore rather than question the feelings she stirred inside me. I cocked my head. *Why can't I be The Closer with my feelings for Goldie?*

I brushed her back with my fingertips, and she leaned my way, relaxing her shoulders. The small movement shot a jolt of adrenaline through my limbs, landing square in my chest.

Chapter Five

Monday, May 10th 10:50 p.m.
Goldie
Max leaned a shoulder against the wall, his head just inches below the sconce lamp outside the door to my room. His gaze shone with warmth and amusement, most likely the effects of the nightcap we enjoyed at the hotel bar. *I like this side of you.* Beneath the hard line of his jaw, a hint of sandalwood cologne rose from his skin. His lips carried the scent of cabernet, and they formed a firm yet soft line like they had something to prove. He dipped his head, and that rogue thatch of hair brushed his forehead.

Does he know how hot he looks?

I sighed on the inside, remembering his sneeze on the walk to the car this evening. *Why do I find something so innately human so incredibly sexy on him?*

I tilted my head, adding that tidbit about Max to the half dozen others I'd squirreled away from my conversations with Sofia over the past few months. It was like playing a game of Connect Four in my head, aligning my observations into neat little rows. *His zodiac sign, dry cleaners, golf handicap, even dog groomer— leaving me guessing about his canine friend...or maybe friends?* Bottom line, I liked facts. Facts were straightforward.

He touched my hand, and my musings fluttered

away. My gaze lifted to his sensuous mouth, its curves daring me to take one taste and walk away.

"Those lips," I said, the words slipping off my tongue.

"Excuse me?"

His question broke my trance. "Oh, Lord. I'm sorry I—"

"Wait. You feel it, too, don't you?"

I hesitated then nodded.

He leaned toward me. "You know, I've been trying to get a read on you tonight, but I'm pretty rusty at all this."

"Let's get one thing straight, Max. There's nothing about you that's rusty."

A smile quirked at the corner of his mouth. "The word means nothing to you because you're young and beautiful."

I crossed my arms over my chest. "You really think a lot about this age thing, don't you?"

He sighed. "I'm thirty-one, Goldie."

"Well, lucky for you my ceiling's a good thirty-three."

He bit back a smile, his eyes growing softer, warmer. "I like you, Goldie."

"I like you, too, Max."

"I really want to kiss you."

"So, what's stopping you?"

"The very real possibility I won't be able to stop," he said with a reverent tone.

Forget Connect Four. Think Battleship, with Max dangerously close to sinking my submarine.

I inched closer, gazing into his eyes. "I think I'll take my chances."

Max brushed my chin with his fingertips, and I leaned into his kiss. My shoulders relaxed, and as his mouth moved over mine, the quiet hum at the back of his throat vibrated against my lips. He deepened the kiss while lifting his free hand to cradle my neck. At his gentle urging, my lips parted, and he drew me closer, sliding his fingers through the hair at my nape. For several silent beats, sharing the same breath, I surrendered to his masterful mouth.

When his lips finally left mine, the hair feathering over his brow made him look like he'd just emerged from a friendly tussle...or a tangling of bedsheets. I blinked up at him, and my good sense fled like a church mouse. A different game-inspired thought popped into my brain.

"Truth or Dare, Max Corda."

He smiled, cupping his hands around my elbows. "Truth."

With my thoughts about him lingering between the sheets, my question was a no-brainer. "Do you sleep on your back or side or stomach?"

"Side. But sometimes I wake up on my back."

"How about when someone's sleeping with you?" I tilted my head, squinting to decipher the expression sweeping across his face.

"Seeing as I've slept alone since my divorce, it's hard to be certain. I've only ever shared a bed with my ex-wife, and before that with James, until he outgrew his fear of thunderstorms."

While Max's admission didn't surprise me, his deferential tone framed a stunning truth. The man before me might ooze sexuality, but he was made of much more serious stuff. He hadn't wasted his high school days sweet-talking cheerleaders in the back seat of his car.

He'd spent his college years committed to his girlfriend, studies, and rowing team…not charming the panties off girls at fraternity parties. *No scattering your wild oats…no fly-by-night hookups.*

"What?" he asked, leaning his shoulder against the wall.

I bit my lower lip.

"*What…?*"

I blinked, recovering my thoughts before they tumbled further down the blackhole of infatuation. "Oh, nothing. Just remembering how the twins used to climb in bed with me when they were little." He raised a surprised eyebrow, and I shrugged one shoulder. "Yeah, I have five siblings. Sage and Billie are twins and two years younger than me."

"Interesting names. I'm sensing a theme here."

"My parents called us their Wildflowers." I raised my hand in a fist, ticking them off one by one. "In age order there's Aciano—who goes by Ace—then there's Hawthorne, or Thorne for short. Next is Primrose—"

"Wait. Let me guess." He rubbed his chin. "Rosie?"

"Good guess, but no. Too cutesy. She goes by Prim." He mouthed an 'Ah' as I continued. "The name suits her. She's a dedicated nurse, kind and gracious, and my greatest friend on the planet." I lifted my fourth finger. "Next comes me, Goldenrod." I paused for dramatic effect, relishing the effect his smile had on my self-confidence. "Then, we have the twins. Sage is eleven minutes older than Bilberry, aka Billie."

"Damn, your names are about the coolest thing I've ever heard." Max reached over to tuck a strand of hair behind my ear. "I like big families, and I was pretty good at looking after my little brother and sister. James was always pushing the boundaries while Jess was busy decorating them. But I can hardly imagine a childhood where I was in the middle of a six-pack of kids."

I laughed. "Yeah, most people can't. Plus, we brought our friends home all the time, and there were the guys working on the farm. Never a dull moment."

He crossed his arms over his chest. "What was it like being the middle of three girls?"

I tilted my head, tossing his question around in my head before answering. Giving responses didn't intimidate me—after all, I was a former pageant contestant. *But this question's different.* Probing yet without being meddlesome. His interest was genuine, and it filled me with a calm confidence I'd never before felt with a man.

"I loved it. Prim was such a caregiver to me and Billie—and to Sage—that I could just relax and enjoy being me. I played with the twins a lot when I was little, but as I got older, Prim and I bonded over swimming and being health nuts. We're both really independent, but we still need that connection with each other."

He nodded then scratched his head, ruffling his hair. "Wait, what were we—?"

"Your sleeping position." I said, finishing his thought. I grinned, adoring this side of Max. He was boyishly charming, but also alarmingly a man.

"Yeah, I'll stick with side. Preferably spooned around a woman who smells like," he said, leaning down close to my neck, "honeysuckle. Or I don't know. Might not sleep at all."

The little thermometer in my girly parts spiked.

"Now it's my turn. Truth or dare?" he asked, smirking.

"Truth."

"Cotton or satin lingerie?"

"A little of both. But either one, they have to be pretty. And I'm an equal opportunity buyer when it comes to color. Care to guess what color I'm wearing right now…?"

He covered his heart with his hand and leaned backward, shuddering.

"I'm killing you, am I?" I bit back a smile. "Truth or dare?"

"Dare," he said, voice raspy.

I reached for the keycard inside my purse and waited several long moments before whispering, "Would you like to come inside, sit down where we could talk better?"

Max gathered a lock of my hair between his fingers and rubbed it meditatively. "That's probably not a good idea."

I felt a frown tugging on my lips. "If it's because of us working—"

"Ahh, no," he said, deadpanning and sliding his hands in his pockets. "It has nothing to do with you working at CDD. I didn't hire you, you don't report to me, and I have no say in promotions at your level. That's Ethan and Dad's job."

"Would you be surprised if I told you I already knew these things?" I asked sheepishly. "I may have read through the policy on workplace relationships…a few times."

He gave me a flirty chin raise. "When?"

I sighed and, figuring it was useless to tiptoe through the minefield I'd stumbled into, kept my tone surprisingly light. "The day after I met you—made for some very interesting reading over my Cobb salad at lunch."

Max smiled and took my hands, giving them a gentle squeeze. "Honest much?"

As I gazed at him, the stark sincerity in his expression caught my breath. "I-I try to be…and not just because it's Truth or Dare."

He moved a step closer. "I feel the same. I'm pretty traditional with relationships, and I already know we're not one-night stand material. This is not just about sex. Nothing would make me happier than to get to know you better."

Wow, I mouthed, staring at him slack-jawed. I took one seriously deep breath to settle my galloping heartbeat. I wanted to cheer and squeal at the same time but figured that would diminish the most beautiful words any man had ever spoken to me. I bit into my bottom lip, trying to find my voice. "I'd like that."

Max reached for my hand and threaded our fingers together. "Good. Now, how about you give me one more, Peach?" He flashed me a glint of white teeth. "A dare."

A whiff of a smile crossed my lips at the endearment. If I wasn't careful, I'd expire right here from sheer bliss. Still clutching his hand, I leaned back against the door. "I dare you to call me in ten minutes."

He drew his brows down. "And…that's it?"

I pushed out a slow breath, hoping I wouldn't regret my next words. "And play me a song you like to have sex to." A quiet pause lingered between us, then Max dropped my hand.

"I can't." His voice sounded crestfallen. "Afraid I don't have one."

My heart hooked at the back of my throat, and I

instinctively reached out to cup his cheeks in my palms. Our gazes locked. *No more chasing dots, Max. Not with me.* I kissed him—and he kissed me back—slowly, deeply.

When we came up for air, he pressed his forehead to mine. "How about we meet in the middle? I'll call you in ten minutes…and we'll talk…and see where things go."

Max lifted the key card from my hand and opened the door. My gaze followed him as he made a check of my suite, and my heart tightened at the protective gesture. He returned and pressed his palm to the small of my back. "All safe."

Am I? I nibbled my bottom lip. *Because I feel like a four-alarm fire right now.*

He flashed me a satisfied grin, then kissed my cheek. "Now lock up behind me."

Chapter Six

Max

Ten minutes. Not nearly enough time to recalibrate my life.

I set a timer on my phone, swapped my dress clothes for a tank and a pair of athletic pants, and stepped in front of the mirror. I ran my thumb over the frayed neckline, regretting in my rush to pack I'd not grabbed a nicer one. *What the hell—it's not like she's going to see it.* I lowered my head and pinched the bridge of my nose. *Goldie's twenty-four. Yeah, I'd say she's expecting a video call, Dumb Ass.*

I blew out a shaky breath against the memory of the one time I'd tried it with Ashley. She hit me with a snarky comeback because my interruption made her shriek during some interdepartmental lecture. So as was my custom at the time, I blamed her reaction on bad timing and eased back into my lane.

My gaze drifted to my backpack on the floor, the book my counselor recommended to me tucked inside. With Andy's help, I was learning healthy relationships can actually benefit from a little lane-switching. *It's not all about cool and orderly.*

In the final years of our marriage, when poker nights with my buddies had increased in frequency and intensity—as had our fishing trips to the Outer Banks—

I accepted Ashley's disinterest as respect for my personal life. Likewise, I took the extensions of her girls' beach weekends in stride, setting reminders on my phone to give MerryBelle her heartworm medicine with breakfast.

I realized our relationship was over when Ashley called me an 'emotional misfit' and cited it as her reason for not wanting to have children with me...ever. She'd not said the words in anger but more a simple matter of fact. I'd spent at least a dozen hours in counseling with Andy to climb out of that dark hole.

My phone alarm pulled me out of my head. *Seventh inning stretch.* I crossed the room and reached for the book in my backpack, flipping through the pages until I found the passage I wanted. *Go beyond what's expected. Delve deeper into your feelings. True intimacy is earned, not given.*

I tossed the book on the bed and turned back to my reflection, hauling in a series of breaths. My sensory radar may have grown rusty from years of neglect, but it was far from broken. Our little game of Truth or Dare had confirmed as much. Goldie made my radar blip, spike, and chirp like a damn techno-symphony.

South of my waistline, the part of my anatomy that ruled supreme wanted Goldie. *Bad.* Yet the parts above it—like the organ hammering away inside my rib cage— would never settle for one night. I'd been dreaming of long, lazy, stretched-out-under-a-moonlit-sky lovemaking since the day we met. Something about the way she'd blushed in the hallway hinted she wanted the same thing.

I reached for my phone and dialed her cell.

****

Goldie

47

My phone buzzed on the dresser. I glimpsed my reflection in the mirror, smoothing the straps of my pink cotton tank top over my shoulders and mussing my hair. It buzzed again, and I grabbed it, knee walking on the bed and snuggling into the pile of pillows at the headboard. I pinched my cheeks. *Wait for it...*

With the third buzz, I tapped accept and Max Corda's face appeared, a dizzying image of hot guy with clover green eyes. His warm hello drew my attention to the stubble on his jaw that seemed to have grown darker in the ten minutes since our little game in the hallway. I returned the greeting and gazed at him leaned against the headboard, bare arm cushioned behind his head. A thousand sparklers sizzled inside my body. *Shit. You're practically shirtless.* I bit my bottom lip softly.

Max cleared his throat. "I can hardly remember my name when you do…that thing with your mouth."

I quickly released my lip, struggling to keep my gaze off his taut underarm muscles. "Let me help. It's Maxwell Lynd Corda." *Yes, I'm a stalker.*

His initial look of surprise faded into a smile. "Thank you. You know, I may need your help tonight with all of this—what are we even calling *this*?" A crease formed across his brow.

"A middle-ground dare."

"Right."

"Foreplay?"

"A man can dream."

I tilted my head. "So can a woman."

Max sighed, something between a cough and a chuckle. "I'm going to tell you something, and I don't even care if you laugh at me."

My gaze softened, and I tucked my feet beneath my

legs.

"Today. Tonight. You, me," he said, waving his finger toward the camera lens, "*this*. I haven't felt so alive in a long time." He cocked his head, making his hair fall to the side. "No, make that ever."

My heart clinched in my chest, and a rush of feelings spilled from my mouth. "I should probably tell you I've had a thing for you since we met. Right there in the conference room, I told myself 'Max Corda is a DEFCON One.' "

He sat up taller. "DEFCON—"

"One. Yes. Means you're a serious nuclear threat to women, specifically me. I can't remember a day since then that I haven't thought about you."

A smile tugged at his mouth. "Really? Uh, how many times a day?"

"Greedy much?" I giggled, recalling his similar line from earlier. I rolled over on the bed with my phone, feet kicked up behind me, giving him a prime time view of my cleavage. "Only happens when I'm breathing."

Max laughed out loud, the rich brandy sound warming me to my toes. He moved suddenly, dragging his phone with him. When the camera refocused, he was stretched out on the bed, propped on his elbow, head resting in his hand. A spray of dark chest hair came into view. *I think my Max-i-verse just flipped on its axis.*

While I recovered my breath, his gaze softened. "Like I said, I want to get to know you, Goldie. I want to know everything about you. And I want—" He closed his eyes for a moment, then opened them. "No, I need you to know me, too. I've never said that to anyone."

"Not even your ex-wife?" I shamelessly put the accent on the 'ex' part.

"She thought she understood me without digging deeper." Max released a slow breath. "And for the most part that suited me fine."

"Right." I dragged out the word, staring at him for several seconds. "Um, will you excuse me for a moment?"

I flipped onto my back, phone screen face down on my belly, and checked my breath. *Max is talking about his marriage, meanwhile I've had only two boyfriends in college.*

I shut my eyes, recalling how the first one was a fraternity rat, utterly useless in the adult world, causing me nothing but headaches. The second boyfriend possessed real magician skills, giving me the disappearing act when he realized a relationship required more cognitive load than reading a list of import beers. In the years since college graduation, Relationship Land moonlighted as a barren desert, and I couldn't help but wonder why.

"Goldie…?"

Max's voice sounded muffled, and after I cleared my throat, I tilted my phone toward my mouth. "Hang on, okay?"

I ran my fingers through my hair. *I'm not wired for nonsense like love at first sight.* I was an environmental civil engineer. I wasn't a poet like my mom. *Holy crap.* I squeaked out a tiny giggle. *Maybe Mom's right and there's something to those sonnets after all.*

"Goldie? You all right?" Tenderness etched Max's voice, and my heart felt close to bursting. If someone had told me a week ago, or even yesterday, I'd have shared dinner and a sexy game of Truth or Dare with my DEFCON One, I'd have doubled over in laughter. Love at first sight? *Yeah, I'm a believer.*

I lifted my phone above my face and gazed into the dark pools of his eyes. "Thanks, I'm fine now."

"You had me a little worried."

I rolled onto my side, leaning my phone on a pillow. "Sorry, I just needed a sec. Now, go ahead. Ask me anything you want."

Max smiled. "Okay. So…do you like cats or dogs?"

Grateful for the soft pitch, I grinned. "Oh, definitely dogs. I grew up on a farm." I paused, waiting for the look of surprise that washed over everyone's face whenever I dropped that bomb into conversation. When it appeared, I added, "Yep, an honest-to-goodness farm with two border collies and a beagle, but I don't have a real pet of my own yet. Apartment rules."

Max nodded in understanding. "You'll have to meet MerryBelle, my Scottie. Well, I share her with my ex-wife, but honestly, I think she likes me best." He leaned toward his phone and whispered, "I give her the best treats."

My body temperature spiked. *I get you, MerryBelle. I like his treats, too.*

"I'd love to meet her." I grabbed another pillow, plumping it under my head. "But until I have a place of my own for a pet, I have to settle for a saltwater aquarium. Fifty gallons. I can't snuggle with my little fishes, but I swear they happy-swim over to me when I walk up."

"It's because you have their food."

"Or maybe they're attracted to my smile," I said, pointing to my mouth.

Max listened while I dished about some of the ups and downs of my beauty pageant experience. Most people presumed it was a glamour show, but I started competing for other reasons.

"I admit I don't know much about pageants, but clearly you did. And you put your talent to good use, saving your winnings for college tuition. I'm impressed." A gleam sparkled from his eyes. "I can see you commanding the room, sealing the deal with your talent and personality. You did the same things tonight with Jack and Leigh. The folks at Shembery Isle had better look out."

I met his gaze. "Thanks, Max—coming from a man whose presence fills a room so easily, your opinion means a lot." I took a deep breath and smiled. "Now it's my turn. Do you like the room warm or cold?"

"Cold."

"Even in winter?"

"Especially in winter."

My thoughts strayed to what Max's bedroom might look like come December…soft flannel sheets wrapped around a king-size bed, covered with a pile of cozy quilts in shades of spruce green and stone clay.

"I love snuggling, and I always like a little fresh air even when it's below thirty degrees. It's the farm girl in me."

"That's it. You're the one for me," Max said brushing his hands together. "I'm taking you to the slopes this winter. Do you ski or snowboard?"

"Does waterskiing count?" While my smile asked *seriously*, his replied *for real.*

"Absolutely. And don't worry, Peach. I'll stick close. I won't let you fall."

He said the words like a promise, and I melted a little on the inside.

And so we continued our conversation, swapping stories for the next couple hours. I told him about Three Creeks, my family's bicentennial farm in central North Carolina where we raised everything from Angus beef cows to alfalfa. I explained how we managed to balance ever-shifting agricultural markets with our history as an active family farm. Despite residential development spreading out from the city, selling it had been unthinkable.

"But Daddy recognized demand for the adjacent land was not going anywhere, so he decided to work with the developers to foster a respectful relationship. He used to brag to our new neighbors they wouldn't find a more tranquil sunrise or sunset anywhere in the county."

I cleared my throat against the nostalgia in my voice. "Daddy was right, and our neighbors loved him. They also loved settling in beside us knowing the farmland wasn't ever going to be commercialized."

I noticed how the corners of his eyes turned down, and I sighed. "Yeah, so my dad passed away my freshman year in college. His heart. Gray Vreeland ate his vegetables, but he enjoyed his red meat a little too much. Dangers of being a cattle farmer, I guess." I attempted a chuckle, failing miserably.

"I'm sorry, Goldie. Sounds like he was a wonderful father and a visionary with protecting his family's legacy."

I nodded. "My brother, Ace, runs everything now, and he's fantastic. My mom's retired from teaching, and he's helped her expand her fresh flower farm into a regular tourist stop. He's even convinced Thorne to temporarily move back home to renovate Old Rambler." At his wrinkled brow, I added, "It's a smaller farmhouse on the property and hasn't been used in years. Thorne restores historic homes and buildings, and he's going to breathe new life into it as a bed and breakfast, event venue thing."

"Ace is a visionary like your dad."

I nodded again. "Ace and I are really close. I mean I get along with all my siblings, but he's the best." I wiggled into a sitting position and held my phone in my hand. "So…that's enough about me. How about you tell me a little about the Cordas."

A smile reached Max's eyes as he told me about his great-grandparents, nineteen-year-old Italian immigrants who came to America in 1922. Their story unfolded like something you'd read on one of those ancestry websites, a devoted couple married less than a year, arriving in New York with less than ten dollars in their pockets. He reminisced about how his great-grandfather changed his name from Cordonelli to Corda on a job application as a repairman in a Manhattan hotel. Once he came on board, Daniel Corda honed his machining skills, and his natural initiative earned him a spot on their electrician's team in less than two years.

"He started his own business at twenty-seven. My great-grandmother, Sylvie, cared for their two sons— ensuring they did well in school—and helped him with the bookkeeping at night. That's how my family began, right there in a two-bedroom apartment in Queens." He ran his hand through his hair, lips turning upward. "Now the fourth generation of Cordas are making their mark all across the country, in every field under the sun."

"Now that's about the coolest thing *I've* ever heard. I think Daniel and Sylvie would be very proud."

"So would your ancestor who got the land-grant

from King George. Damn, that's a really long time ago."

I grinned, knowing if it weren't for work looming in a few hours and sleep tugging at our eyes, we might last until dawn. I hid an impending yawn behind my hand.

"It's getting late, yeah?" Max sighed, stretching his arms. "But God, this has been the best night."

"I've never had a more wonderful evening." If I could, I'd shout the sentiment from the rooftop.

"If I start to nod off tomorrow, you'll be there to nudge me, right?"

The stars couldn't possibly be more aligned than they were in that moment, and I blew Max a kiss through my phone screen. "I will. Promise. Sweet dreams, Max."
I know mine will be.

Chapter Seven

Wednesday, May 12th 9:20 a.m.
Max

"Nature-based solutions are messy, folks. Humans, much like our animal friends, find purpose in constantly rethinking, reshaping, and rebuilding their surroundings." I paused for a sip of water, then clasped my hands around the edge of the podium and leaned toward the microphone again. "Adaptability is the thing I love most about urban planning and design. We're always searching for the sweet spot between flexing and stabilizing, sustaining and renewing, in every design decision. In my opinion, whether it's a metropolis balancing its biodiversity or an emerging township preserving its delicate ecosystems, 'mess' is best because it means nature is helping us take care of business right here on Earth. Right here in Shembery Isle."

My gaze moved across the faces of town aldermen, planning engineers, and residents gathered in the assembly hall, then it swung to Goldie seated in the front row. My chest swelled, her rapt expression nailing me every time.

After spending practically every hour with her for the past two days, I'd unlocked a few of Goldie's secrets…like how she lightly tilted her head to the left to detract from the annoying cowlick in her hair…and how braces and headgear may have corrected her overbite, but the way her eyes softened at the corners? *Yeah, like in that smile right there...?* That one was all for me.

I cleared my throat to keep from blurting out, *"I'm crazy about this woman!"* and instead offered, "And now, I'm going to turn things over to Goldie Vreeland, who you all know is your lead project design engineer. Get ready to be amazed, folks. She's going to show you just how perfect 'messy' can be."

****

Several hours later, after Goldie nailed her presentation with the town council, she and I left work in the rearview. We swapped out our business casual for comfortable casual, though her sleeveless linen top tucked into straight-leg jeans screamed sexy. I took her hand, leading her outside the resort and toward the rental car.

Goldie sighed. "You really aren't going to tell me?"

I opened the passenger door for her. "Impatient much, Ms. Vreeland?"

"Control much, Mr. Corda?"

The most adorable, frustrated scowl appeared on her face, and I chuckled under my breath, unable to remember a time I'd had this much fun planning a surprise. I squeezed her hand. "Hardly. I've never felt so *out* of control. But in this, you're going to have to trust me, Peach."

As I took the highway exit toward Charleston, I pulled out a baseball cap from behind Goldie's seat. "You might want to put this on. The sun's pretty bright this afternoon."

She studied it, then cast me an airy smile. My gaze flicked toward her, and dawning washed her face. "Baseball?" She wiggled in her seat, peering out the window at the signage outside the stadium. "Wait. Are we going to a Clam Diggers game?"

I nodded once, a little surprised at how quickly she'd figured me out. Though I'd been a rower on an athletic scholarship in college, I played baseball in youth league. With Dad's experience, he coached most of my and James' teams. We both loved the sport even if we hadn't inherited our dad's gift for the game.

I rubbed my knuckles over my lip. "I hope you don't mind. Jack and Leigh asked if we'd like to join them. They're bringing their kids, too." After pulling into a parking spot and killing the engine, I turned toward her. "When I was explaining to you the other night how my family and friends talk a lot of baseball jargon, I remembered you saying you'd only been to a few high school games—"

Goldie pressed a finger to my lips. "Are you kidding me? I love sports and kids. It's perfect...you're perfect."

I leaned forward, kissing her senseless. *Correction.* She was kissing *me* senseless, for the only thought rambling around in my head these days was how she took me to places I couldn't find on my own. I'd never been much of a romantic dreamer. The risk outweighed the reward every time. But with Goldie, I was willing to pay the price for dreaming. *And then some.*

When we eased back, allowing a breath of air between us, she put the cap on her head. "So, how do I look?"

I thought of a dozen ways I wanted to answer her, each one a punctuation mark on my growing feelings for her. But I stay focused. "Too good, Peach. You're about to short stop my heart."

She liked my answer, inching closer and pressing a

smiling kiss over my mouth. "Don't worry about a thing, Max. I'm a first-string catcher."

****

Nothing fueled my soul like a competition and spectacular stadium food, and I soon learned healthy options were a real thing at a Double A baseball game. Goldie spotted a food truck with grilled chicken tacos and seasoned corn on the cob parked beside a hotdog stand, and we ate alongside our friends.

A couple hours later, with a final score of six to four, the Clam Diggers pulling out an eighth inning two-run homer to take the lead, the seven of us piled out of the stadium with arms full of kids and souvenirs. My gaze flickered to Jack who held his two-year-old daughter, Janie, tight in his arms. Good thing, since she was as wiggly as a puppy—and twice as adorable.

Their oldest child, Nate, walked between Goldie and me, each of his hands in one of ours, reeling off a story about his tee-ball game last weekend. *He's definitely inherited Jack's flare for storytelling.* Leigh had charge of their middle son, Charlie, who after fussing for the last inning was now sobbing. The sound stopped all of us in our tracks. Leigh kneeled in front of her son, hands on both his shoulders, soothing him with soft words.

Goldie and I exchanged a glance, and when Nate dropped my hand to scratch his cheek, I nudged my chin in Jack's direction. She nodded, and I went to stand beside Jack. Without even a sideways glance, he deposited Janie in my arms and joined his wife, kneeling alongside her. I hitched the pint-sized girl higher on my hip, and Goldie eased in beside me, still holding on to Nate.

"Hey," Goldie said, taking Janie from me. "I think

you should take Nate over to his parents. He says he knows why Charlie's crying."

Memories of being the oldest kid in the family washed over me, and I met Nate's troubled gaze. I walked him over to his parents.

After a few tense moments of conversation with Nate, Jack raised up, plowing his hand through his hair.

"What the actual f—" Jack clipped the word before leaning over to whisper something in Leigh's ear. Jack hugged her, then pressed a kiss to Charlie's forehead. He gently gathered his son in one arm and grabbed hold of his wife's hand with the other. "We think Charlie stuffed some peanuts into his ear."

"What..? That's impossible—we didn't have peanuts." My expression must have shifted from confused to stern because Goldie's hand tightened around mine. My tone often came out more serious and pointed than I liked. It was the natural by-product of a life spent managing people and things. I shook my head and croaked, "I'm sorry, Jack. I-I don't understand."

"Yeah, well, with three kids under the age of six, things rarely make sense." Jack chuckled, but the sound was anything but light.

****

Goldie

After seeing Charlie's stuffed animal, torn at the seam and filled with small white pellets, Max and I shared a look of belated understanding. *Peanuts.* With our promise to take care of things, Jack and Leigh drove off with their son to the emergency room.

If Max Corda had been my DEFCON One for months now, he vaulted off the charts after this rescue at the ballpark. Within minutes, he rose to the pinnacle of 'hot-dad' gorgeous in his tee-shirt, jeans, and baseball cap. He looked completely at ease carting around a couple of kids, strapping Nate and Janie into the car seats we'd moved to our rental. Max had them calmed and settled, singing "Old McDonald Had a Farm" before we pulled onto the highway. He had a voice like one of those old-school singers from my grandmother's album collection, and even if the lyrics were corny, I was about one verse away from falling seriously in love with this man.

It was near dark when we arrived at Jack's home, a sprawling brick ranch flanked with tidy sidewalks and magenta crepe myrtles, tucked away at the end of a cul-de-sac. While Max assumed kid patrol in the den, I poked around in the kitchen, pulling together the ingredients for a baked mac and cheese for the children. After finding some grilled chicken and greens in the fridge, I whipped up a salad, drizzling it with a honey balsamic vinaigrette I made from ingredients in Leigh's spice cabinet. As we sat together at their dining table, Janie in a highchair and Nate seated with his superhero plastic plate and fork, Max said a blessing for our food and Charlie's quick recovery.

The scene reminded me of home, the all-too-short period of childhood where we laughed and squabbled, teased and debated everything over family suppers. As an eighth-generation farmer, my dad roasted anything he could fit on his king-size grill, and my mom created the best salads from her vegetable garden. The mood in the Vreeland kitchen was always spirited, but we never lost sight of what mattered most in life—family.

I turned to Max, folding my arms on the tabletop, and giggled. "Oh, now *that's* a good look for you."

Janie clapped her hands in glee.

Nate's laugh bubbled up from his belly and spilled out his mouth.

Max grinned, wiping his thumb over the goatee of melted cheese Janie had dabbed on his chin. "Fingerpainting my face with food I can handle. But I steer clear of little girls and their fingernail polish."

I paused, holding my fork of salad inches from my mouth. "Sounds like you speak from experience."

"I was twelve when Jess was three, and she got it in her head my babysitting duties included her painting my nails." I watched Max's broad shoulders shudder ever so slightly. "She was such a girly girl and had me wrapped around her pinky—still does—but I had to draw the line on that one."

I unfastened Janie from her seat and placed her on my lap, wiping her hands with a fresh napkin. "Ditto for my big brothers. But I could get the twins to play pretend with me anytime." Janie surprised me, cuddling into my chest, her weight instantly warming me. I hugged her closer. "Sage liked wearing my flashy scarves and pantaloons and pretending to be a pirate. He'd come up with the craziest stories for us to act out—and he was only four years old."

Max helped Nate climb onto his knee, wrapping an arm around the boy's waist. "He's the screenwriter?"

I nodded. "Yeah, I'm glad he's back in North Carolina. The show films in Wilmington, and if it's a hit, he'll get to stay for a while."

"What's it about?" He mumbled the question around his last bite of salad.

"It's a CinaFlicks series. Young-adult angst set against a small-town coastal backdrop. A little paranormal influence, too."

"Huh, sounds like something Jess would like."

I nodded. "I watched the premiere. They've got a great-looking cast."

"As in young, hot, and full of sexual tension?" He raised his glass to his mouth, his Adam's apple flexing with each swallow of water.

On the heels of that sexy image, I grinned. "Funny, but that sounds a lot like you."

He drew his brows down, uncertainty creeping into his expression. "Maybe the sexual tension part…but I'm not young or hot."

"Uh, hello? You fly your own airplane…?"

"Technically, it belongs to CDD."

"Yeah, but you're a *pilot*, which is without question, totally hot." I smiled at Janie, thumb wedged in her mouth, then turned to Max. "So, when did you learn to fly?"

"Dad's a pilot. He let me steer the plane for a couple of seconds when I was eight years old, and I was hooked. I got my license right after college and take off every chance I get."

"Flying with you felt amazing. I'll never forget it."

He tousled Nate's hair, studying the short, faded sides and fawn brown spikes on top before looking my way. "Thanks. Not everyone feels like you do."

He didn't have to say who didn't like flying with him. Ashley's influence lingered in the creases around the corners of his eyes. I wished I could erase all his unpleasant thoughts, but his mind wasn't some whiteboard. I decided it'd be better to fill his head with fresh experiences, warmer memories. *With me.*

I moved to stand, keeping Janie tucked against me,

and squeezed his shoulder. "I'll go anywhere with you, Max. Just say the word."

He gazed up at me with a look equal part resolved and maybe even...*hopeful*?

I sighed, amazed at how Max and I had eased into this natural rhythm in just three days. I mean, his tilted smile still made my pulse flutter, but my nerves no longer flew into a frenzy when he entered the room. I could walk by his side with confidence, knowing he'd shorten his stride to accommodate mine. And whenever we talked, his gaze softened...like he actually cared about what I was saying.

My breath hitched as images of the Charlotte skyline and CDD's corporate office crept into my mind. Soon we would have to leave our little bubble of sandy shores and simple pleasures. I tamped down the thought. *Though I don't know exactly what* this *is, I'm damn sure not ready to let it go.*

We shared a lingering look before he reached for my hand and kissed it.

Emboldened, I said, "Until then, just let me know if you'd like me to show you exactly how young and hot you are."

"I can't decide if that's a truth or a dare."

I tilted my head and smiled at him. "A little of both. But most of all, it's a promise."

Chapter Eight

Wednesday, May 12th 11:35 p.m.
Max

My gaze drifted from the sports channel documentary on television to the heads sleeping on each of my thighs. I tucked the blanket under Nate's chin with my left hand and smoothed back Goldie's hair from her cheek with my right. I rubbed a lock of her hair between my thumb and index finger, studying its wave in the shadowy light. It was the color of butterscotch, but in the sunlight, I'd seen it dance with glints of gold…just like her name. I loved the way her hair bounced—even with the cowlick she detested—and beckoned me to lose my hands in the weight of it.

I took in a deep breath and released it slowly. Ashley and I shared a past…*but could Goldie be my future?* I flexed my fingers, releasing the lock of her hair, recalling the list of differences I'd doodled on my tablet this afternoon while Goldie wowed the townspeople of Shembery Isle.

Ashley: petite, thin, blunt cut brunette hair, only child, predictable, categorized and alphabetized every staple item in our pantry, and squirreled away chocolates in her nightstand.

Goldie: tall, slender yet curvy, long wavy-gold hair, one of six children, prepared and thorough, spontaneous, and hadn't met a fruit or nut she didn't like.

What I hadn't had the courage to decipher this afternoon, and found myself wrestling with all evening, was how well I actually fit with Goldie. *Am I what's best for her?*

I grabbed the TV remote to lower the volume, then leaned back on the sofa, putting my arm over my face. I'd fallen for Ashley almost from the moment we met at prep school in Virgina. We were sixteen, and I'd never known anyone—besides myself—who could awaken at the same time every morning without an alarm clock. Unfortunately, I was young and failed to pinpoint that too much similarity might be a bad thing.

In our youth, Ashley had matched me in every way, intellectually and socially, and she charted a seamless path for our future. She researched universities with the highest ranked business and engineering schools—and rowing teams—completed our applications and had us committed to Tech by Christmas of our senior year.

Ashley wasn't my first kiss, but she was the first woman I made love to. *The only woman so far.* While our marriage failed the test of time, infidelity wasn't to blame—I was sure of it. As we invested more time in our careers, we simply grew apart, swapping marital intimacy for financial reward. After a few years, sex— which she doled out like a ration to a third-world orphan—became a Saturday night ritual, sandwiched between a couple glasses of wine and some rom-com on cable. MerryBelle became our connection, the little symbol of life bridging a lot of gaps for us.

As Nate shifted under the blanket, I thought about the leather bracelet in my pocket but knew pulling it out was too risky. Ashley had made it in folk art class and given it to me for my birthday. She threaded a blue glass bead onto a leather strap, added seven beads to spell 'A+M4EVR,' then closed it with a red glass bead. The colors symbolized our birthstones, sapphire and garnet. The beaded band had hung on my key ring for years, and when it began to age, I started carrying it in my pocket to keep it safe.

When I caught myself twisting the edge of Nate's blanket between my fingers, I looked up and sighed. Some men jingled coins in their pocket. I toyed with my leather band. I dropped my hand on the sofa cushion, cursing myself for keeping it close even after the divorce. Andy had questioned my decision, too. And after more than a year of counseling, I'd still not uncovered a reasonable explanation.

The vibration of the garage door lifting snapped me back to the present. As the deadbolt lock snicked open and a weary but relieved threesome walked into the den, I squared my shoulders and met them with a smile.

"Sorry we're so late, but when is an ER ever empty...?" Jack held a sleeping Charlie in his arms, and Leigh stood beside him. "Thanks for taking care of the kids."

"Absolutely. They were great." I tilted my chin toward Jack. "How is the little guy?"

He pressed a kiss on Charlie's hair. "Much better with three foam peanuts removed."

"No shit? Three?" I all but choked on my shock.

Leigh walked over and carefully lifted Nate into her arms. "I know, right? Thank God he's okay, but I can't wait to ask him why he did it. Anyway," she said, whispering over her shoulder as she padded toward the hallway, "thanks for everything, Max. We love you...and Goldie, too."

Jack stepped closer, his gaze flickering to where Goldie remained asleep. "Your girl's a sound sleeper."

"Like an angel. She and Nate went lights out about an hour ago."

"Thanks for letting him stay with you. He was probably a little spooked about what happened to his brother."

Leigh soon reappeared beside Jack and took Charlie off his hands. He whispered his thanks, then sat in the chair across from me.

His gaze fell to the coffee table. "Now there's a fresh do-over for coffee filters and watercolors."

I chuckled with him at the garden of hand-crafted flowers scattered across the tabletop. "Something Goldie and her twin siblings used to make when they were kids. Some sort of props for the skits they'd dream up."

"Janie loves to play pretend." He leaned forward, forearms on his thighs, hands clasped between his knees. "And don't let Nate fool you for one second. Sure, he swings the hell out of a golf club, but he also whips around a play sword like King Arthur himself."

His description roused images of me and my younger brother, James, when we were kids, racing our motorcycles through wooded trails or working out at batting practice. And after Jess arrived, the Corda home was never the same. She sprinkled her adorable brand of whimsy—painted fingernails and all—into our lives.

Maybe all kids play like this. I rubbed my index finger over my brow, attempting to mask my self-consciousness. I sure as hell didn't know—and probably never would. I lowered my hand, rubbing the curve of Goldie's hip.

Jack's gaze followed my hand, then swung back to

me. "Not exactly how you thought you'd spend your night, huh? Sorry all this spoiled your evening."

I smirked. "Are you kidding me? I've loved being here with Goldie and your kids…in this home you've made for yourself." I lifted my chin in the direction of the kitchen. "Have you seen your refrigerator, Jack?"

He stammered something unintelligible under his breath followed by a hollow, "I guess so?"

"Crayon-colored pictures for Mother's Day, a calendar with 'Nate's Kindergarten Graduation' scribbled with a silver marker…and some invite to a dinosaur-themed birthday party?" I swallowed a painful laugh. "Jack. Buddy. It's a fucking shrine to what we're put on this earth to do. Find love and if you're lucky enough, make babies. Brilliantly amazing and…imperfect little people."

Jack dragged his hands back and forth through his hair. "Yeah, ones who stuff foam peanuts in their ears and scare the hell out of you."

I sighed sympathetically. "I'll have to take your word for how much that part sucks. I gave up on the idea of having children a long time ago."

"When you were married to Ashley, yes. I get it. I guess kids weren't in the cards for you guys."

"No," I corrected. "It had nothing to do with chance. The choice was Ashley's, her decision over her body."

Except for Goldie's soft breathing, stunned silence hung in the air between us.

"Why didn't you ever say anything?"

"It's not something I liked thinking about, let alone discussing."

"Not with anyone?"

I shook my head.

"You're one strong bastard. I don't know how you did it."

"Miserably. I did it miserably, and about the time we separated," I said, lifting a hesitant gaze, "I started seeing a counselor."

Jack air-pointed his finger at me. "Best damn decision you could've made. You still seeing her—or him?"

I nodded. "Him. Andy Howell. And yes, every Wednesday. Just not this—"

"Wednesday," Jack said along with me before adding, "Today you indulged in a little home run counseling with your girlfriend—"

"Goldie's not my girlfriend."

Jack quirked an eyebrow. "Ahh, but she could be…" He settled back in his chair. "And you also engaged in a bit of role-play therapy with your *could be* girlfriend and my two other kids who've only stuck their fingers in their ears so far."

Jack's poignant summary triggered something warm in my chest. "And for the past few days, I've been living under Goldie's spell. She's incredibly smart and has this way of drawing people into her circle. Like she's made to mingle or something." I rubbed my hand over her hip, and she sighed softly.

"All excellent qualities for a wife and mother. You need to forget your history of reruns, make something fresh and original. You could get busy with Goldie and in no time," he said smiling and gesturing with a sweep of his hand, "be living in paradise like me."

"You make everything sound easy."

"Trust me, it's not. But it's so fucking worth it." He scooted forward in his chair, planting a hand on each knee. "I'll email you my bill in the morning."

I barked out a laugh, and the sound roused my sleeping angel. As Goldie blinked and turned the corners of her mouth into a sleepy grin, I heard Jack rise from his chair, chuckling under his breath.

"Lock the door on your way out. And remember...get busy, Corda."

Chapter Nine

Thursday, May 13th 8:15 a.m.
Goldie

"Where have you been...? I can't believe you've ghosted me all week. Wait, wait..." The sound of Sofia's heels clacking on the floor lifted from the speaker on my phone, bouncing off my bathroom walls. "I've got to sit down for this."

I leaned forward to wipe a smudge off the mirror. "What're you talking about? We've been texting."

"Schedule updates do not count, and you know it," she said, and a few moments later she chimed in. "Okay, I'm good. Now give me the details."

I grinned, not needing to see my dear friend to picture how she'd be perched at her desk, foot wagging while she unwrapped some fruit pastry roll. "Have you ever fantasized about someone then found out the reality is so much better?"

"You remember what I told you. Roman nose, long fingers..."

"Well, I can't confirm *that*, but I'm hopeful. I mean, I told Max I'd been scoping him out for months." I paused, makeup brush in my hand. "But you know, from some of the things he's said, I think he noticed me, too."

"Uh-huh. I told you Max doesn't miss a thing. I've seen his credit card charges this week, too. Thibodeaux's, something from a sports shop in town, and a baseball game yesterday?" I could tell she was chewing by the way she mumbled her words, then cleared her throat. "Glad you two have squeezed in some fun this week."

I recounted the past three days while applying powder and blush.

"Wait. Are you telling me you guys took care of Jack's kids, then you fell asleep with your head on his *thigh*?" She blew out a low whistle. "D'you know how hot that sounds—you and Max off playing house together?"

I dropped my makeup brush in my bag and stared at my reflection in the mirror. "I drooled on his khakis, Sofia. I left a cold wet circle of my saliva on his pants."

"Dangerously close to his junk, huh? Too bad you were asleep."

I slapped my hand over a gasp, picturing her saying all of this while sifting through her inbox and clicking her ink pen.

"And don't think I didn't hear that little gasp thingy. It's my job to say out loud all the things you're thinking about Max."

I grinned at the 'nailed it' ring to her voice and dropped my hand to my hip. "It may have been embarrassing, but I've got to say he's a pillow I could *really* get used to."

"Can I ask you something, Goldie?" She waited before continuing, "Do you want kids one day?"

I sensed a deeper layer in Sofia's question, and I thought about it for a beat. *She knows something.* Was she trying to protect Max? Was she trying to gauge the level of my commitment to my career? Was she hoping to let me down easy when I said 'yes,' and she'd have to tell me Max doesn't want them?

I gazed at my reflection in the mirror, sliding my hand over to rest on my belly, knowing my answer without any doubt. "Yeah, I do. Someday."

"Good to know."

I could practically hear the seconds ticking by, and finally interrupted the silence with a desperate, "Because...?"

"Because Max wants a wife, kids—the whole enchilada. He's wanted a family for a long time," Sofia said in an uncharacteristically serious tone.

I swallowed hard. "I-I didn't know, not for sure anyway. I guess I wondered why they didn't—"

"It was Ashley. She didn't want children. It's one of the biggest reasons they split up."

The vision of wicked sea serpent Ashley invaded my thoughts, and a shiver climbed up my spine. It must have been awfully sad to be with someone—without really *being* with that someone—for so long. After that experience, I could understand why Max treaded cautiously through the dating waters.

I reached for my jar of styling pomade and sighed. "I think Max would be an amazing father." As I smoothed the gel over a few errant strands of hair, I wished my feelings for him could be tamed so easily. "The other night, Max asked me about my family and where I grew up. He told me he likes big families, too. Do you think...?" *No. It couldn't be possible.*

"Uh-huh. He's interested, Goldie. Max is definitely interested in you. And you know what else?" she asked, smacking her lips while crumpling a plastic wrapper. "I've never known him to stick around the office at lunch...until you and I started hanging out together."

I tightened the lid on the jar and set it on the counter. "And why am I just hearing this now?"

The sound of her giggle lifted in the air. "I didn't want to freak you out. I know you're tough and all, but you didn't need to think too much about this. Better to dive on in."

"Oh, I've taken a dive all right. Right off the highest platform." I stepped away from the sink to snap my hoop earrings in place before continuing. "I'm talking emotionally though, not physically. I mean, we've kissed a little. The scariest part is I've shared more of myself with Max than either of my old boyfriends combined." I detected the question in her silence. "But when and if we ever get to *that*, I promise I'll be safe." The silence continued. "Sofia? You there…?"

"Sorry, girl. You know how I brain-fart sometimes."

I sensed hesitation in her voice and urged her along with an "Uh-huh…?"

She grumbled softly. "I was just thinking about how there's this great see-saw kind of thing happening with you and Max. You balance each other out, the highs and the lows. You could be so amazing together. Way more than I expected when I sent you off to buy condoms."

"Yeah?"

"Yeah."

Hearing the conviction in her voice, I stood a little taller.

"I mean, a roll in the sheets would be amazing, but if you guys truly connected…and your relationship turned into something lasting…"

If I were a cartoon right now, there'd be pink puffy hearts circling around me. I shook my head, then reached for my lip gloss, the trio of silver bangles on my wrist tinkling. "I hope you're right, Sofia. Max is the most incredible man I've ever known." My tone softened. "When we talk, it's like secrets and stories come pouring out of us."

"Listening is a huge turn-on for a man like Max. He's such a fortress for everyone in his life." I heard the sound of papers rustling on her desk. "Yeah, yeah, people hear him and follow his orders. But I don't know who actually *listens* to him, you know? A man needs a woman he trusts to listen."

I pressed my phone to my cheek, sighing my agreement.

"I get Max and Ashley were *all that* when they were young, but as grownups they were a hot mess, him chasing around her dots. Hell, I knew the marriage had caved years ago when he started having me choose her presents."

"No way. Like birthday—"

"Yep, and Christmas and Valentines, too. And because I'm one hell of a shopper, he always came off looking good." She punctuated the last word with sass. "But seriously, avoidance is not in his nature."

I was bobbing my head up and down when I realized Sofia couldn't see me. "Oh, yeah. You're absolutely right. We're getting to know each other, and I think—or I guess I hope—we're going to find something special together. But for now, we're mostly colleagues. Kissing colleagues? We're definitely not *together* together."

"Be patient with him, Goldie. I've seen the way he looks at you. It's different, you know, in a good way."

"Good in like he won't ask you to pick out my presents?" As I pulled my hair into a ponytail, I winced but not from the elastic band. *This is Sofia, stupid.* Even if this thing with Max—whatever *it* is—never materialized, I was sure we'd remain close friends.

"Exactly," she said, giggling. "And speaking of gifts, I'm wondering if one of us shouldn't be buying Ethan a present for getting appendicitis this week?"

"Yeah." I tried to chuckle at the irony but fell short. Even though I'd already gotten a wellness text from Ethan, I listened to Sofia's update. Ethan would be in the office on Monday. Max and I were cleared to fly out tomorrow afternoon, coming back to work—and *whatever*—on Monday, too.

I gazed at my reflection in the mirror, resisting the pageant smile tugging at my lips. *Do not panic.* Other than Max being my DEFCON One, and the fact I was one tiny slip away from falling in love with him, what was there to worry about? I closed my eyes and groaned a quiet sigh. *I don't know, like face-planting when we get back to reality and he rejects me?*

"So, tell me what you're wearing," Sofia said, grabbing my attention.

I described my outfit—short-sleeved white blouse belted into fitted gunmetal gray pants, and white sneakers.

"Those cute-as-hell platform ones?"

"Yep."

"And underneath?"

I instantly remembered Max's flirty question and my response. "Very pretty white satin."

"Uh-huh, it's every woman's secret weapon."

We shared a laugh, then I heard sounds in the background. "Hey, I can hear you've got company. I should get going, too. We've got a site visit and assessment review starting in an hour."

"Go show them how it's done. And remember, be patient with Max…and safe."

I ended the call, closing my eyes, trying to shuffle around the events from the last four days. While he'd surprised me with the dinner at Thibodeaux's and baseball game, his gentle heart—and finesse with a fine game of Truth or Dare—had stopped me cold.

I opened my eyes with the realization Max simmered like the old radiator at my grandmother's house. Strong, sturdy, and reliable, I loved that old heater despite its little clanking noises. I felt a squiggly wiggle take a turn inside my chest. *Like I think I love Max, too.*

I lowered my gaze and peeked inside my cosmetic bag, the slogan on the unopened box of condoms glaring at me. *When safety counts, count on premium protection.* I zipped the bag closed and with a huff, grabbed my work satchel and slid it over my shoulder. *Too bad those blasted things don't protect hearts.*

Chapter Ten

Thursday, May 13th 3:40 p.m.
Max

I'd spent the better part of the morning gazing at Goldie's tush—which filled out her pants beautifully—while we traipsed through the worksite of one of Shembery's planned agro-environmental gardens. A zoning engineer and landscape designer had fallen in line with her, and my position some ten feet behind them provided me with an unfettered view of her mesmerizing hips.

Before we reached the turn on the pathway, a sales representative latched on to me, droning on about pipes, fittings, and water flow capacity. I nodded my head at regular intervals, mindful to note the specifications impacting our design decisions.

Goldie strolled along the trail peppered with underbrush and roots without faltering, and afterward, glided down a lunch buffet line at the town's recreation center. *White blouse spotless, ponytail bouncing, cheeks rosy.* In contrast, I sported a splattering of mud on the legs of my khakis and gray half-moon shadows under my eyes. *It sucks when you wear the evidence of your late night on your face.*

After we'd gotten back from Jack's house, we spent two hours teasing and talking over a video call. The image of her drowsy eyelids and soft smile on my screen had ransomed my thoughts all day.

Planting my fist against my cheek and leaning on my elbow, I turned and glimpsed Goldie seated to my right in the town's board room. I watched as she took notes, fingers waltzing over the keyboard as the speaker clicked through a slideshow about natural stormwater infrastructure opportunities in the town. At one point during the presentation, she gathered her hair with her hand and draped it over one shoulder. I flexed my free hand around my knee, wishing I could wrap my fingers around her thick ponytail. Antsy, I reached for the complementary notepad and ballpoint pen on the table and scratched out a sentence. I nudged the note into her left pinky.

She lowered her gaze, reading. *"I hope you're concentrating on this better than I am. For Ethan's sake."* She wedged her pen between her teeth, launching a thousand wicked thoughts in my head. I waited while she wrote her reply then slid the paper back to me. *"Distracted, are you? Hm, I wonder why..."*

I bit back a chuckle at her flirty heart emoji punctuation at the end of the sentence. *Yeah, why indeed.*

After the meeting adjourned, we made our way back to the resort. Inside the elevator, I leaned back against its mirrored walls, enthralled by Goldie's summary of our progress thus far. When the doors parted, I ushered her out, still charmed by her chatter but stopped short at her door, scooping her hands into mine. I leaned forward, brushing my lips against her ear.

"Are you blind? Trust me, the guy from the nonprofit was hoping for more than your 'assessment of the hydraulic schematics.' "

Goldie leaned back. "And what about the sales rep

with all her talk about 'corrugated steel pipes' and 'sealed fittings'?" She rubbed her fingers over the buttons on my shirt, and my stomach tightened. "She was making it pretty clear she wanted a seal around *someone's* pipe."

Her words sent a shiver rocketing up my spine. I'd engaged in more sex-infused wordplay this week with Goldie than I had in my entire life, and it made my head swim.

"The way she wiggled in beside you while we toured the gardens? Shameless." Goldie lifted her pert nose in the air and inhaled. She put her hands on her hips, shaking her head. "I'm afraid you're going to have to change shirts. I like your scent, not hers," she said, a hint of tease in her voice.

I snaked my arms through hers and pulled her close. "When that douchebag mentioned touring the coastal 'wetlands' with you, I wanted to punch him." Sharing never suited me. *No one steals the oars from my damn boat.*

"Hm," Goldie said with a sassy smile, pressing her thighs together in an inherently sensual way. "That's actually a very accurate description."

I nuzzled the curl of her ear. "What're you doing to me?"

"I'm trying to make myself irresistible." She released a soft sigh. "Is it working…?"

I looked left and right, then pulled her flush against me. Her breath hitched, and my arousal intensified. "Does *this* answer your question? Hell, it's three thirty in the afternoon, and all I want is to take you to my room."

"And do what with me?" She rubbed her palms on

my chest, her breath tickling my neck.

I pressed a kiss to the top of her head. "I wouldn't want to rehash a middle-ground game of Truth or Dare."

She lifted her gaze, biting her lower lip, a bloom of color rising in her cheeks.

A gritty noise escaped my throat, one I hardly recognized. "Christ, I know I should be taking the high road right now. Keep to my plans for a walk on the beach, a nice supper…" I pulled her lip down with my thumb, releasing it from her teeth. *These are all I want to taste right now.*

"You do know they're calling for showers this evening." She peeked at me from underneath her lashes. "Remember when we were talking last night, and we both agreed there's nothing better than pizza and cold beer?"

A smile inched across my face.

She lifted on her tiptoes and whispered against my ear. "I bet a slap resort like this has kick-ass room service."

"Yeah. Slap." I swallowed hard, hating my quick, desperate response. Though we'd flirted for much of the week, this current exchange had kickstarted things. I was so worked up I couldn't help but reach for her. A breath later, I found my voice, speaking slower, squeezing her hips. "Bet they'd deliver our pizza under a giant silver dome lid, a couple of frosty mugs for the beer. We could even—"

The elevator down the hallway dinged, the sound floating in the air between us, but my focus remained on Goldie and my need to get closer to her. "Another dare, Peach?"

She shook her head, lifting her chin. "No. Truth."

Holy God. Never had I heard so much expressed in so few words. As the elevator door opened, I laced my fingers between hers and brushed my lips over her ear. "Go get what you need from your room. You're coming with me. All night. I'll wait for you here."

Chapter Eleven

Thursday, May 13th 4:05 p.m.
Goldie
After swishing mouthwash in my mouth, grabbing
the essentials off the bathroom counter—*yes, my bag
with the box of condoms*—and stuffing them inside a
small duffle, I gazed at my reflection in the mirror. I took
in a handful of cleansing breaths. I'd never said so little
to a man and gotten so much. This truth was Max and me
and every fantasy I'd ever had about him, but it skirted
close to reality, too. *We can* be *a couple, Max.* I bit back
a tiny squeal, dusted bronzer over my cheeks, and dashed
out the door, stopping short at the frame of hot guy.

Max linked his fingers with mine and led us to his
suite. Once inside, I turned around in a circle, certain my
face mirrored one of those giant stadium screens,
projecting emotion to the world…to him. He lingered in
the foyer, his gaze following me as I strolled through the
galley kitchen and into the living area. His suite—
outfitted with luxurious lighting and a cozy sectional
sofa—dwarfed mine. He'd upgraded, as he'd done with
most things this week, every decision purposeful…and
personal.

As Max walked toward me, the space between us
disappeared. He encircled me in his arms, tucking my
head beneath his chin, my nose pressed against his
Adam's apple.

"You fit me like a puzzle piece…a piece that's been missing for a long time." He squeezed me tighter, his warmth sinking into me. When he lifted my chin and sealed his lips to mine, a sun shower burst behind my eyelids. He slid his hand to my nape, cradling it as though it might break. Our tongues met, teasing and tasting. He explored my mouth with gentle strokes, arousing my senses while anchoring all awareness in the kiss.

He slowly pulled back. "I need to be clear with you. I don't want a one-night stand, and I mean it. If you don't feel the same, it might be best—for professional reasons, if nothing else—we stop while we still can."

A heady thrill zinged through my body at the depth of his tone. I steadied my breath. "You, please order room service. Me," I said, pointing a thumb over my shoulder, "I'm going to duck inside the bathroom for a minute. And as for us…" I lifted on my toes and kissed him square on the lips. "Us is what I want, Max. Right now, and then some."

He smiled. "All right, then. I guess I have just one question for you." His hands fell to my hips and squeezed gently. "What do you like on your pizza?"

Some hours later, after savoring a garden veggie pizza and a couple pale ales, Max stood behind me on the balcony. I breathed in the briny sea air, pulling his arms tighter around my waist, wanting his touch branded on me.

He dropped his chin on my shoulder. "I have a confession to make."

His words rumbled through his chest, vibrating against my back. I resisted the urge to flinch and hugged him closer.

"I've been attracted to you for months, Goldie. Painfully so. Kind of paralyzed by it."

My mind stuttered, finding it impossible Max, in all his alpha-maleness, would struggle with anything, least of all women. "But you've been dating. I mean, a few weeks ago you took the lifestyle editor from that magazine—" *Shit.* He turned me around in his arms, and I peeked up at him, biting my lip. "Yeah, about that…you know Sofia's my best friend since I moved to Charlotte, right?"

He nodded, the twinkle in his eye lightly encouraging.

"Well…I may have overheard her making dinner reservations for you and the editor—"

"Damn, you're adorable." He touched my cheek with the back of his knuckles, running them along my jawline. "A fundraiser for the hospital, that's all." When my shoulders relaxed, he continued. "Believe me, I'm well aware of your friendship with my personal assistant. I've found it damn near impossible to concentrate on my work when you two huddle-up at her desk for lunch."

Wow, Sofia's right.

"I hope you didn't mind my hovering."

I shook my head. "Not at all. But were we too gossipy?"

He chuckled softly. "No, I liked it. Sofia's like a sister to me. Your little lunches gave me a window into your world without having to put myself out there."

"But if you were attracted to me…why didn't you do anything about it?"

"Dates to charitable events—things my sister would attend with me if she wasn't spending her college semester in Scotland—are one thing." He pushed out a slow breath. "You are something else entirely."

I narrowed my eyes, head tilted.

Max studied me, a smile in his eyes, lips thoughtful. "You're twenty-four years old. I'm thirty-one. Forget I have a shitty track record with relationships, even if I've only had the one—"

As he plowed his hand through his hair, mussing it in that roguish way that always made me smile, my heart tightened in my chest. *Here's this crazy-gorgeous guy, intelligent and accomplished...and as uncertain as a teenage boy with a squeaky voice.*

"—and then Ashley had a thing at the university this week, and I'd promised to take her. I got pissed when Dad and James cornered me into taking Ethan's place."

I lowered my head, tucking a strand of hair behind my ear. "Yeah, I-I saw you at the office when you were waiting for the elevator. You didn't see me. I mean, I was there by the break room, but like you said...you were pissed."

Max lifted my chin, waiting until I met his gaze. "I panicked because this perfect opportunity to spend time alone with you scared me shitless."

His confession reminded me that while he was my DEFCON One, he harbored insecurities same as the rest of us mere mortals. "And now...?"

He sighed a heavy beat. "For the first time, I'm trying to live my life on *my* terms. I hope I don't come off like some conceited ass, but truth is, I don't like change, and my emotions tend to run pretty deep. I was with my ex-wife for fifteen years, but my feelings were never like they are with you. You're real and honest. I feel so alive when we're together." The pull of his voice, the methodical stroke of his hands on my arms, wrapped around me like a cozy blanket. "I don't have to guard my feelings with you, or worry I'll fall short."

A frown twisted across his face. "Jesus, this is all coming out wrong. It sounds like I'm looking for an easy way out, but I'm not." He pulled me into a hug, whispering over my ear, "I want to get to know you better and make you happy, Goldie. Please know that."

I swallowed a tiny knot in my throat and whispered into his neck. "I believe you. We don't have to put a name to this yet. But please, Max." I pulled back, needing to see him—for him to see me—before my nerve dissolved. "I might die if you don't touch me tonight."

Max dipped his head and touched his lips to mine. Sweet heat swirled in our kiss, and he slid his tongue between the seam of my lips, delving deeper. As I moved my hands over his shoulders and locked them around his neck, a sigh escaped me. He curled one hand around my waist while settling the other on the curve of my ass. We lingered in each other's arms, lost in a haze of kissing sensation, then he slowly pulled away. His gaze simmered, the green of his eyes both potent and powerful, and he took my hand, leading me inside.

He closed the balcony door, and my senses awakened to our surroundings. He leaned a hip against the back of the couch while I circled the room, gazing first at the wireless speaker on the bar, then at the bottle of champagne on ice. My attention drifted to a silver domed dish, not the one from our pizza. I peeked inside, and then at Max. As I lifted the lid to reveal fresh strawberries, a smile ghosted across his face.

"You're spoiling me, Max."

He swiped his finger across his phone screen, and a

soft melody filled the room. "That's the plan."

I tilted my head. "Wait. Is this *the* song?" I strolled toward him.

"Could be." He met me halfway and threaded our fingers together. "I felt inspired. Instead of checking my email over coffee this morning, I made this playlist. I couldn't settle on just one song."

"Let's make a pact—right now." As he lifted his eyebrow, I continued. "In the interest of full disclosure, I think we should have a go at every song you've got here before we choose our *favorite* song for sex."

"But you don't know how many there are."

I recognized that look and tone. *Firm jawline, smooth negotiator.* All his cool confidence made me wonder how he acted outside of work. Did his polo shirt stay tucked in when he was tossing back a pint with his friends at some sports bar? Or did all of that melt away when he relaxed, leaving an intensely sexy, thoroughly real male? *Like how he is when we video chat?*

That image snapped me out of my revelation. "Well, if my super-sensitive Max Corda instincts are correct, there will be approximately...eleven."

"I had no idea you had a superpower...outside of making me horny as hell." Smiling, he released my hands and stepped over to the bar, popping the champagne and pouring it into two glasses. "So, why eleven?"

"Rhymes with heaven."

"So does seven."

"Nope. Not nearly enough time." I accepted the glass he offered and sipped. "The way I see it, the average length of a song is about four minutes, right?" He nodded. "But that multiplied by seven is only twenty-eight minutes." I wagged my finger at him. "But eleven songs would give us about forty-four minutes. And being the sexy, practical man, you are, you'd go with eleven, making sure we had plenty of time for…" I slid my index finger between my lips, my girly parts tingling from months of fantasizing about Max's fine package.

He set his glass on the bar top with a thud and dragged his hand through his hair. He cupped the back of his neck, releasing a haggard breath before meeting my gaze. "Christ, Goldie. You'd do that for me? After I took care of you, of course."

I placed my glass beside his and moved in front of him. I glanced up at the line of his shoulders and higher to the smooth skin of his neck, then clipped my gaze in a heated rush. While I imagined he seldom explained himself to anyone, I sensed he wouldn't mind fielding a few questions…even difficult ones.

"Has it been that long?"

"An eternity."

His admission made the bump bumps in my chest speed up. "It has been for me, too."

Max stared at me as if I was some secret, uncrackable spy code.

On a solid breath, I continued. "Look, if we're going to do this, I want you to know my number. It's two. In college, I had sex nine times with two boyfriends…and that was three years ago." I bit into my lip, adding, "Does any of that bother you?"

"No." He dipped his head, rubbing his knuckle over his lip. "But doesn't my number bother *you*? I think it's been part of my hesitation about dating again. Most women want a man with experience."

"Well, I'm not most women, and I think you just

need the right partner."

"You think of me like that?"

I nodded. "How about you?"

"You're all I think about."

The corners of his eyes softened, and a warmth spread through me. This sexy virile man hungered for tenderness and intimacy. He exuded command and control, yet kept his needs hidden. Until tonight, I'd been a lightweight in the sex department, no man having ever highjacked my body and senses so completely.

"Sex doesn't make the man, Max." I stepped closer. "But the man definitely makes the sex. Guys my age have no clue about what makes me tick…anatomically or emotionally." I traced my thumb around the button on his shirt, quietly adding, "And I know this because I've never had these feelings before."

Max pulled me in for a kiss, soft and tender. "Then it's been a long time for both of us. I only want to please you, Peach."

I steadied my fingers around his belt buckle, the metal tinkling as I flipped the prong from the frame and let the leather straps hang at his waist. I rubbed my hands over his rippled stomach, feeling his muscles twitch, the air between us charged with anticipation.

"Twenty-one." He brushed the back of his hand over my cheek. "Songs to love you."

A smile tugged at my lips. "And why twenty-one?"

" 'Cause being with you makes me feel like I've got the best hand at the table. Like I've won the jackpot."

I wrapped my arms around his neck. "That's it. Forget three. Twenty-one is officially my new favorite number."

He laughed then lifted me in his arms, and I kissed

his cheek.

Once inside the bedroom, Max lowered my feet to the floor. I gazed across the room, light flickering over the bed and shadow dancing on the walls.

"Candles. Very nice."

"Preparedness is a virtue for me."

I worried my bottom lip. "And protection?"

"I've got this."

Max unbuttoned my blouse, dropping it and my pants to the carpet, and stepped back. He ran his finger from the base of my throat, through my cleavage, and lower to my panties. I closed my eyes, head falling to one side, his gaze warming my skin.

"Satin." Appreciation laced his voice.

"You like?" I smiled inside, but then sexy undergarments made me feel beautiful and strong.

He answered with a sexy hum of approval, his hands moving up my back and unhooking my bra. It fell to the carpet, and my breasts tingled against his touch. He cupped them, thumbing my nipples to aching hardness, and my breath escaped in tiny stuttering gasps. I mourned the loss of one hand to my breast, only to revel when it slid lower and covered my ass. My hips flexed in rhythm with his hands.

"More, Max. Please…"

He bent to kiss me, reassuring me with the driving pressure of his lips, then moved his mouth along my jaw, blazing a trail of kisses up to my ear. He gently scraped his teeth over my earlobe. "Demand much?"

"Come much?" I don't know how I managed such a flirty comeback with my desire skirting so close to the edge.

He chuckled into my ear. "Not nearly enough. But I

have a feeling you're about to change that."

Max tore the duvet from the bed and stepped me backward into the mattress. I scooted up, loving how his hard-on tented his pants. I reached for him, but he shook his head, grinning devilishly. He slid my panties down my legs and tossed them aside. As his gaze moved over my naked body, my skin turned to gooseflesh.

"Fuck. You're even more beautiful than I imagined." He crossed his arms, grabbing the ends of his shirt and yanking it up and forward, the neckline pulling his hair over his forehead. He dropped it on the floor and climbed onto the bed. "And I imagined a lot."

I purred a smile and parted my legs, only he spread them further. His kisses began on my inner thighs then ghosted toward my throbbing knot. I shifted beneath him, and he teased me with his nose.

"My bossy, brainy, beautiful girl." He circled me again. "Is there something I can do for you?"

Bossy, brainy...what? I vowed to throttle him later. *Much later.* "I'm dying, Max. I mean dyinggg..."

And then his lips touched me *there*, and I trembled. I needed a moment for reality to replace the dream. I reached down and ran my fingers through his hair. *Max Corda is here...with me.*

He murmured soft words that vibrated against my sensitive skin, then moved his tongue in teasing circles. My head turned into the pillow, and I raised my arms above my head, surrendering everything to him.

Max flicked the tiny bundle of nerves, coaxing the frisson growing there. Lost in a place of dizzying bliss, I moved my hips with the rhythm of his tongue. He covered me with an openmouthed kiss, drawing every sensation thrumming through my body to that sweet pressure point. I scarcely recognized my voice, sounds rasping and spilling from my mouth as I peaked, quivering against him. He cupped my behind, pulling me closer, swirling his tongue inside me. He waited for me, for the wave of pleasure to subside, before lifting his head.

"My God, you're beautiful when you come." I felt his grin against my hipbone before he kissed it, then he crawled over me, caging me with his body. "I could watch you like that all night."

"You've been the star in my fantasies for some time. For this to be happening…well, it's almost too—"

"Much," we said together.

Positioned above me, keeping his weight on his forearms, he pressed kisses along my collarbone and murmured, "I know the feeling."

My skin tingled with his words, and when he lowered his head to my breast, my world shattered. He teased my nipple with his lips, circling and caressing, before he drew on it deeply. My fingernails dug into his biceps as he lowered one hand, stroking a rhythm between my legs in time with his magnificent tongue. Sensations jetted through my body, leaving my limbs tingly and warm. His sandalwood scent lifted from his skin, and I breathed it in, delirious, surrendering to another release.

In the aftermath, I held him against my breast, his ear pressed against my thrumming heart until he shifted his hips, and his belt buckle poked my hip. I muffled an ouch, and we chuckled together, then I wiggled out from under him and onto one elbow.

"These," I said, my gaze darting to the pants stretched tight over his arousal, "have got to go. Please let me see you."

Max rose and turned, his pants resting low on his hips, his black briefs visible. I wanted to tug on the waistband to see if he had those two sexy dimples above his tight ass. As he reached for his phone to raise the volume of the music, my gaze lingered on the breadth of his back and shoulders. My toes curled in the sheets. *Got to love he's a rower.*

He pivoted back to me, and the view was stunning, like when the velvet curtain lifts on a stage. The span of his chest, his muscle-streaked stomach, and the thick bulge bucking against his pants arrested me. Before his masculine beauty completely stole my breath, I scooted toward him, kissing him softly on the lips.

****

Max

Goldie kissed with the same honesty she brought to everything. We melted together, and as I explored the soft contours of her mouth, I wondered if she liked her taste on my lips. *Christ, I do.*

After a few sweet moments, she broke the kiss and lowered her gaze, running her finger along my waistband. Anticipation hummed through my body with the song filling the air. She sat on the mattress and placed her feet between mine. I flexed my hands at my sides, counting the snicks of the teeth in my zipper as she lowered it. I closed my eyes, taking measured breaths. When she freed me from my confines, her fingers stroked my heated length. I jerked my eyes open and stared at the cloud of tawny hair poised before me.

Ashley and I'd had sex, but since the early days of our marriage it lacked intimacy. Along the way I'd rationalized intimacy as a perk, not a necessity…a filet mignon to a flank steak. Oral sex morphed into a forbidden fruit, something rare and savored in small quantities. While dating and in the honeymoon years, we'd indulged, usually after one too many drinks on a date night. But things changed, and sadly, when ignored for too long, even the sweetest fruit rots on the vine. In short, I'd become adept at assuaging my biological needs and skilled at ignoring displays of affection between other couples.

I brushed Goldie's cheek with the back of my hand, and she lifted her head. *Well, you've blown my rationalization to hell.* With her lips parted, her breath rushed over me, making me harder. Making me needier. Making me vulnerable in a way I'd never been before. *How can you shatter me, and make me whole, all at the same time?*

She stripped off my pants, then cradled me in her palms, stroking my erection. "My God. You...you're stunning, Max." The raw edge to her voice tipped the scales, and I groaned between gritted teeth as she enveloped me with her mouth. I'd gone without for so long, the hole inside me was a fucking crater. Her tiny suction sounds lifted through the air, mixing with the beat of the music surrounding us. The backs of my legs thrummed, passion taking hold, growing, clawing. The pleasure threatened, and I struggled to prolong my release.

"Goldie. Damn," I rasped. "You feel unbelievable. I can't take much more..."

My gaze fell to where her soft sensual lips encircled me, kissing up and down my shaft. I groaned when she cupped my sack and took me deeper. *Holy hell.* I thrusted forward, mimicking the motion of her mouth, skirting close to the edge.

"I'm gonna—God, I can't stop. I can't pull—" In response, she grabbed my ass with her free hand and drew me closer. The last of my defenses fell away, and my climax came barreling down my spine. I gazed down at her, the silky curtain of her hair surrounding me, and groaned my pleasure. My body quaked, my release washing through me…and into her.

If I lived to be one hundred, I knew this memory would stay with me. I'd recall her mussed hair and plump lips, our scents fused together, and the sensual songs of sex in the air. I took her hands and brought her to standing, her softness pressed against my hard-lined torso. I cupped her chin, our gazes locked, and I saw no regret reflected in her eyes. I traced the bow of her lips with my thumb, and she wrapped her arms around my waist.

I lowered my head, kissing her softly while easing her onto the bed. My hands cradled her back and neck as she settled in amongst the mound of pillows. A new song lifted in the air, and a smile stretched across her face. I drew her against me, my chest a pillow for her head.

"Hm, I like this one…" Goldie snuggled in closer, sliding her leg over mine and rustling the sheets between us.

"When I hold you like this, I'm lost. Completely. In you." I pushed out a sigh, equal parts awe and raw emotion. "What we just shared, what we gave to each other, is something I don't take lightly." Her breath hitched, and I bent to kiss the top of her head. "Hey, are you okay?"

"Yeah, I think so. It's just, you don't know how— you can't begin to—"

"D'you remember what we talked about?" I felt her cheek rub up and down over my chest. "I'm not some player. You're the first woman I've wanted since my divorce." I dug deep into the maelstrom of feelings raging beneath my sternum before continuing. "I haven't always been present in my relationships, Goldie. I know how to protect the ones I care for, but I'm not so comfortable letting them inside. I want to be a better man." I squeezed her tighter. "A better partner."

"Oh, Max." Her voice carried over the music and landed square in my chest. She raised on one elbow, her expression brooking no objection and turning darker in the flickering candlelight. She smoothed her hand over my shoulder, then lifted it to my cheek. "From the moment I met you, I knew you were special." She traced the line of my jaw with her index finger. "You're brilliant and decisive, and demanding, yes. But you're also kind and generous...nurturing and loving."

I eased onto my side and cupped my free hand on her hip. I tamped down the urge to kiss her, feeling the moment too intimate to brush aside. She stirred a hunger inside me, and I was a greedy brute. "What makes you think those things?"

A soft pink infused her cheeks, and she peeked at me through her lashes. "You're my DEFCON One, remember? Pretty much means you've been my sole focus..."

I quirked my brow.

She released a sigh. "Since we met."

A smile crept across my face.

"I know it's pathetic, right?" she said, bunching the sheet in her hands and rolling onto her side. "So, I volunteered at the hospital's BestLife festival because

Sofia *might* have mentioned you're on their board of directors."

I adored how she squeaked out the word 'might,' and I plumped the pillow beneath my head, kissing her nose, urging softly. "Go on."

"And after I heard you and Ethan talking about how desperate they were for an instructor to teach swim lessons, I *might* have—"

"Wait. I heard about this. You're the new mama of the Guppies class, aren't you?"

She nodded. "I've been a certified lifeguard and instructor since high school."

"I am too—or well, I used to be. In college I was—"

"Captain of your rowing team." She chimed in, squeezing my bicep. "Um, I may have neglected to tell you I'm a little obsessive. I like information, and I couldn't help myself. You're much too interesting."

I chuckled at how easily Goldie surprised me. At every turn. And I'd never been so happy to be thrown off my game. I pulled her into my arms, loving the way she fit me. As her hands glided over my chest and across my stomach, my pulse shot up a notch. I'd always thought I gave as good as I got, left everything on the field. I was discovering she was a go big or go home girl, too. I suspected I'd do just about anything to be with her like this tonight…and always.

I lifted her chin, brushing my lips over hers, and whispered, "I really like how you think you have to tell me that. Trust me. I get you. And I believe you get me, too."

Chapter Twelve

Friday, May 14th 4:40 a.m.
Max

I recognized the ring tone instantly. I groaned, groping for my phone on the nightstand and cursing my decision to leave Ashley's number in my favorites. When I reached it too late, I swallowed a sigh of relief. After reneging on the tenure banquet, I'd been dreading talking to her. My fingers twitched, and I gazed at the clock. This was early even for her, and though I wasn't expecting anything pleasant, somehow I couldn't see her chewing me out between her morning yoga and hazelnut coffee.

Goldie rubbed her toes against the back of my calf, the movement sending a warm rush over my skin. I peered over my shoulder at her hair fanned over the pillow, hands tucked under her chin. I rolled onto my side and pressed my lips to her cheek, loving the way her soft sigh filled the air between us. We'd shared a night of intimacy even though we stopped short of intercourse. We decided together our first time should be at home…at my place…in my bed.

My phone rang again. *What the hell?* Shrouded under a veil of uncertainty, I slipped out of bed and strode across the room, closing the bathroom door behind me.

I pressed the phone to my ear. "Hey. Yeah, so um,

I'm sorry I had to miss your banquet last night."

Instead of Ashley's fire and brimstone, the sound of yips and hiccups reached my ears. Her words came rushed but clear, clipped.

I grabbed a towel and knotted it around my waist. "Wait. Slow down, Ash." As I listened, my stomach began a slow crawl into my throat. "Her heart? But I thought she had gastric—" My jaw locked into a hard line with her last statement. *MerryBelle's gone, Maxie. Our baby's gone.*

I couldn't find my words. They'd vanished along with the last living remnant of my marriage to Ashley. The puppy I gave her for our first Christmas together—the gregarious little terrier with the silver bell collar I hoped might nudge us into starting a family of our own—had died in her sleep.

I scrubbed my hand over my face while Ashley preached to me about missed signs and regrets. She didn't call me an emotional misfit again, but I sensed the accusation hanging between us.

My heart tightened in my chest. Had I failed Ashley...and worse, MerryBelle? Because even when we'd forgotten how to love each other, MerryBelle still loved us. *Unconditionally...but not without end.*

The sudden silence from the other end of the phone had me shaking my head. "Sorry, what was that last part? Yeah, what you said—" Tucking my phone between my ear and shoulder, I opened the shower door and sighed, drawing on some hidden reserve of compassion. "Of course, honey. We had so many wonderful times together. Whatever you need, Ash, I'll be there. Yeah, I'll see you soon."

After a pause, she whispered goodbye, and I placed

my phone on a hand towel beside the sink. I braced both my hands on the bathroom counter, head bowed, and groaned a breath. *God, I'm gonna miss you, girl.*

I recalled MerryBelle's first visit to my new place, one of four spacious condominiums renovated inside an old Charlotte mansion, Bladen House. I set up a space for her in the corner of the master suite and covered her bedding with a couple of my old sweatshirts. I worked from home the first week she stayed with me, letting her sniff her way across the hardwood flooring and commit every scent in the English-cottage garden to memory.

I'd purchased the condo near the end of my marriage, proclaiming the property was a wise financial investment—not a complete lie—but I knew better…and so did Ash. As the ever-predictable protector and planner, I was hedging my bets against a future where I'd no longer live under the same roof as my wife. I could see a day coming where we'd settle for co-parenting our spirited little Scottie between our refined rustic ranch in the suburbs and my everyday spacious condo in the city.

I straightened, my gaze swinging to the bathroom door. Goldie—the sum total of everything beautiful and kind and comforting in my life—lay sleeping in my bed on the other side. How could it be in less than a week, I needed her like the air in my lungs? I sighed, reached over to turn on the faucet, then climbed in the shower.

****

Goldie

The mattress moved with Max's weight, but the real shift in the room had come with the ringtone from his phone—you know, the music where the great white shark swam over and took a chunk out of the swimmer? *Has to be his ex-wife.* At first, I pegged Max as the unlucky surfer, but a niggling in my gut had me wondering if I might really be the one in danger. *Does Ashley call him every morning?* My fingers dug into my pillow. *Is this some lingering ritual from their marriage, like sharing the same bathroom sink and bottle of mouthwash?*

They shared nine years of marriage on top of six years of dating. I tossed the number around in my head. *Holy crap. I was nine when he met her.* He'd been in a relationship with Ashley for more than half my life…

I sighed softly, burrowing deeper under the covers. As one of six kids, I'd mastered the art of fake sleeping, and when I peeked between my lashes, I found Max's gaze glued to his phone screen. As I watched the fine form of his ass disappear into the bathroom, I groped for courage in the bedsheet tangled around me.

Another handy thing I'd learned from my siblings was how to snoop. My feet landed on the floor, and I stood, draping the sheet around my body. I swallowed a sigh and tiptoed across the room to the mirror, combing my hair with my fingers. His voice rumbled in low tones, so I moved to the bathroom door and leaned into it. The fact he wanted to speak to Ashley privately stung my nerves.

"Of course, honey. We had so many wonderful times together. Whatever you need, Ash, I'll be there. Yeah, I'll see you soon."

The swoosh of blood running between my ears made me shudder. The gentleness—hell, the *intimacy*—in Max's voice made me nauseated. Tears stung my eyes.

With the sound of running water and the shower door clicking shut, my gaze drifted to the half-empty bottle of champagne and glasses on the table, then to my clothes scattered on the floor. The candles were dark and cold, and the bowl of strawberries empty. The playlist that'd held so much promise last night had ended hours ago. I wiped the corners of my eyes with the back of my hand. I needed time to gather my wits. I stepped out of the sheet and into my clothes, then tapped out a text to Max.

—Hey! Gone to grab a shower, too. And pack. Text me when you're ready to go to the airport.—

I bit into my lower lip while pressing send, then snatched my bag and made a beeline for my room.

Chapter Thirteen

Friday, May 14th 10:40 a.m.
Goldie

Max flew the plane toward Charlotte, his gaze shifting methodically between the instrumentation panel and the sun-streaked sky ahead. He wore his pilot's headset like a crown—level and steady. I studied his profile, my thoughts wandering back to the last time we'd shared this cockpit, his green eyes flashing over me as we traded snacks and innuendo before take-off.

And what about last night? He'd searched my face, my lips, as though he couldn't tear his gaze from me.

Today, heavy brows topped clover gray eyes, and after wrapping his aviator sunglasses around his ears, Max had hardly glanced my way. How could he act so stoic, all prepared and in control, while I was easily teetering on the brink of emotional Armageddon?

I adjusted my headphones over my ears and slapped on my nothing-gonna-stop-me-not-even-heartbreak smile. It, along with the contest trifecta—the walk, quick pose, and sassy turn on stage—had always kept me afloat. I thought about how I'd polished my talent all those years ago, playing my grandmother's dulcimer and earning scholarships to offset my college expenses. Pageants taught me resiliency…and the lifesaving five-minute drill for judge-perfect hair and makeup. I'd never encountered a conflict—or pair of three-inch heels—that could do me in.

After hearing a succession of flap noises coming from the plane as we taxied down the runway—which Max reminded me were nothing more than shifting gears and wind currents—we'd taken to the air without incident. The engine hummed in the background, interrupted only by occasional sounds coming from one of the dozen gauges on the dashboard.

Blip...fuddle, wuddle, duddle...blip.

Funny how a few days ago, these sounds had barely registered in my brain. I sighed, guessing my mind had been engaged in other more *important* things? Like studying the way Max wrapped his hand over the throttle, knuckles bent, controlling the stick with smooth, fluid movements.

My gaze fell to where his palms were now, wrapped around the control wheel. Max had really nice hands, and after the multiple orgasms he'd given me last night, there was no question he knew how to use them. *And his mouth, too.* Suddenly that place between my thighs got all tight, and I wiggled in my seat.

"Hey, you okay over there?" Max asked with barely a sideways glance.

Damn, I hate my traitorous body.

He'd removed his headset, so it now circled his neck. I nodded then allowed my gaze to move across his profile. I had to wonder if I was the cause for the crease on his brow. After his little talk with Ashley, had he decided I was some kind of unwanted, unwelcome baggage? Did the little twitch in his jaw signal regret? Knowing Max Corda and his protective instincts, he was probably deep in thought this very moment about the best way to pitch me to the curb without leaving a mess.

I removed my headphones and let them drop to my shoulders. *I'm not a rotten banana peel you can toss in the compost bin, Max.* I turned toward him and opened my mouth, but what came out was a simple, "Yeah, I'm good. How about you?"

"Me?" His voice lifted even though we were clearly alone inside the plane. But if he was thinking about his earlier conversation with Ashley, then that'd make three of us sandwiched in here.

I smoothed my palms over my yoga pants, cursing myself for eavesdropping on him in the first damn place. There was simply no soothing the sting of what he'd said from behind the bathroom door. *Whatever you need, Ash, I'll be there.*

Max reached over and took my hand. I held my breath and waited—for his flimsy explanation, a heartfelt confession, or some other sign he trusted me with the truth.

"I'm fine, Goldie."

I blinked over the pain stinging my eyes. He had been calling me Peach.

But that was before the phone call.

I summoned my contest smile again, untangled our fingers, and slid my sunglasses higher on my nose. Oh, how I wished I was anywhere, *anywhere* but here.

I flipped up the straw on my water bottle and brought it to my lips. I peeked at Max as I swallowed, damning the sun for highlighting his cheeks and jawline so perfectly. How was I supposed to learn my lesson—from what had obviously been nothing more than a cheesy business trip hookup—when sex rolled off this man in waves?

I'm not some player. You're the first woman I've

wanted since my divorce.

I took a long swallow past the sadness in my heart, letting his words sink in. While I knew he hadn't lied to me last night, I still wanted more than sex with Max. I'd been infatuated with him for months and, after finally acting on our attraction, craved a chance to see where things might go. But most of all, I was holding out for intimacy and trust in a relationship. I sighed, fairly certain that was something a guy who snuck off to the bathroom to take a pre-dawn phone call from his ex-wife couldn't give. I wasn't angry so much now.

I just feel really sucker-punched confused.

After we landed a short time later, embarrassment quickly replaced confusion, crawling over my skin. Thankfully, in a move part self-preservation and part cowardice, I'd used the drive service app on my phone to call for a car. After what I'd been through today, I couldn't handle Max driving me to my apartment.

I didn't realize until I slid into the back seat of the driver's car how my cheeks were hurting from so much smiling. I lolled my head back on the seat and breathed in the citrus scent coming from a freshener clipped to the air vent. For this resilient pageant slash farm girl, it was time to concede. Max Corda, with his broodingly sexy grin, effortless charm, and shitty relationship past, had totally done me in.

****

Max

I sat on my sofa with a box of cheese crackers in my lap and tapped out another text to Goldie. I read and reread it…then blew out my cheeks, backspacing over the words like I'd done with the previous dozen attempts. I sighed. I'd never put so much damn thought into a text to a woman. Not to Mom, Jess, my dermatologist, Sofia...definitely not to Ashley.

But this was Goldie. *Enough said.*

I crouched over my phone, thumbs hovering over the screen. I wanted it to sound like me when I messaged her for the first time since, you know...*last night.* I didn't want to say anything too pushy, too suggestive, too casual...too *anything.*

I groaned, then tossed my phone on the empty cushion beside me and tipped the box to my mouth. As I crunched on the last of the little square crackers, it became pretty fucking clear I wasn't so sure who I was anymore.

Most days, I was a son, grandson, and big brother. I worked for CDD, being the best president and civil environmental engineer I could be. *For my family...for Dad.*

I set the box aside and leaned forward, elbows on my knees, chin against my chest. I listened to the sound of my breathing, concentrating on the steady in and out, just like my counselor had taught me, until I could lift my head.

And on rough days, I was this childless, divorced, work-driven thirty-one-year-old guy without a date to whatever charity obligation popped up next on his calendar. I gazed at the green and tan plaid dog bed I'd moved from its spot by the fireplace to the far corner of the den. *Add dogless to the list, too.* I rolled my shoulders and reached around to rub the back of my neck. *Yeah, just don't hold on to Merry's things for too long.*

I came off the sofa and fished the leather bracelet out of my pocket, rubbing the frayed edges between my thumb and index finger. I held it up to the TV and watched the light shimmering through the beads. Cheap beads. *Only I can't seem to let go of them either.*

I shoved it back in my pocket and headed into the kitchen, grabbing a beer from the fridge. I took a long swallow then made my way to the sofa, leaning back and crossing my bare feet at the ankles.

But I have good days, too. Thanks to counseling, Andy was helping me reframe my thinking around my health, family, and friends. He'd reminded me these were blessings, and for too many years I'd just checked them off like appointments on a calendar.

And then there're the days with Goldie. I yanked the hem of my T-shirt from my jogging pants. I did the math as I pulled on my beer. I'd known her for eighteen weeks. I felt like I needed to start a new count though, to signify the change in our relationship. I held the neck of the bottle and turned it slowly on the arm of the sofa. But was it a real relationship—like so fucking real I could trust it? Trust her…?

The longer I thought about it, the more uncertainty crept over my shoulders and up my neck, setting up house in my head. I wanted to just be myself with Goldie, but after she'd bolted out of my bed while I was in the shower this morning, I had to wonder if she'd seen the real me and decided to take a pass.

I raised the bottle to my lips, drank, then lowered it to my knee. I shook my head. *No fucking way.* This total head-spinning transfer of energy, from the time I left Goldie in my bed to when we met up in the hotel lobby for check-out, had made zero sense. She'd gone from peaceful sleeping angel to smiley chatty parakeet in the span of a few hours. *I know your smile, Peach.* Lips that curled softly at the edges. Lips that plumped and darkened with my kisses. But today, she'd grinned with the same perfect mouth, but with none of the warmth.

When I'd asked her if she was okay this afternoon, I purposely didn't meet her gaze. True, I was piloting the plane, but mostly I was afraid if I did, I'd see regret in her eyes. She'd been wiggling around in her seat the whole flight, and when she wasn't wearing that phony smile, she'd kept her bottom lip wedged between her teeth.

My stomach had fallen when Goldie answered with a simple 'fine,' but then it flipped when she turned my question around on me. The pressure of her gaze made my cheek twitch, and I flexed my hands around the control wheel.

There'd been a beat of silence as I considered being brutally honest, telling her how badly I wanted her, wanted to be buried inside her, breathing in her vanilla honeysuckle skin. I wanted her to know she'd be staying with me tonight so I could do just that.

I also wanted her to tell me what happened, tell me to my face that I just wasn't the man she thought I was. But my words had crowded against my lips, and I ended up giving her the same canned response she'd given me.

"Fuck this." I gulped down what remained of my beer and set the bottle on the coffee table. I raised my hands, cracking my knuckles one by one, then grabbed my phone. Striving for a calm I sure as hell didn't feel, I began typing.

—Hey. I know it's late. Call me if you're up. Thought maybe we could talk, play a little truth or dare.—

I didn't reread it. I didn't add any emojis either. I never did that shit, so why start now?

I pressed send and waited for the little dots. I actually prayed for a solid minute to see them pop up on my screen.

Nothing.

I dropped my phone on the sofa and made my way to the kitchen for another beer. Since the text I was praying for was the elephant waiting in the *other* room, I grabbed a couple slices of bread and stuffed them with slices of turkey and provolone. By the time I'd added a dill pickle to the plate and settled back into the sofa, a good eight minutes had passed. I put my plate on the coffee table, uncapped my beer, and tapped my phone screen.

Fucking elephant's still in the room.

Chapter Fourteen

Saturday, May 15th 8:15 a.m.
Max

I woke up and went on a run, trying—and failing—to get into that space in my head where reason rose above emotion. Mid-morning, I stopped by our vet's office. As I carried Merry's small coffin to the trunk of my SUV, my eyes stung with what I dismissed as an overabundance of spring pollen…which only reminded me of a particular wildflower by the name of Goldenrod. Recalling my promise to Ashley to do whatever she needed, I let out a groan of frustration, then threw my car in gear and headed toward her house.

I found my garden tools right where I'd left them over a year ago, in the back left corner of the shed behind the wheelbarrow and some stakes we once used for our tomato vines. I tucked the shovel under my arm, carried the coffin to the backyard, and placed it in the shade of the Japanese maple. After digging a hole several feet deep, I buried our MerryBelle.

Shoulders sagging, I crouched over her grave, breathing in the resinous smell of freshly packed soil. I watched a dragonfly land on one of the dozen azaleas I'd planted that first spring. My gaze flickered to the trellis I built the following year—Ashley's roses still clinging to the wooden slats—then drifted to the cobblestone path winding through the flower beds. I spied the oak trees we'd fallen in love with all those years ago still standing guard over the lawn, though dandelions speckled the grass now. *Perfect space for a swing set, a batter's net…and a treehouse, for sure.* I hesitated, pressing a fist to my forehead. *Only nothing's ever for sure.*

I stood, a soft breeze curling around the collar of my polo shirt. I reached inside my pocket and pulled out the leather band. I studied it in the sunlight, a hollow emptiness settling in my chest. The ink was fading on the bead with the letter A, making it look more like an H. I rubbed my thumb over the red bead, noting its more orange color now. *It's from a lifetime ago, Max. Get over it.*

The door to the screened porch creaked then banged shut, and I turned my head. Ash's traditional rose and lily perfume lifted in the air as she moved in beside me. She wrapped her arms around my waist, and I held her. Her arms were thinner than the last time I'd seen her—at Mass on Easter Sunday. She pressed her cheek to my chest, and her shoulders quivered. Her tears left a cold spot on my shirt—right over my heart—and the finality of everything sank in. This was goodbye to Merry and our home.

But did we ever really have a home…?

I drew my gaze to the brunette head pressed against me. *Nah, we were mostly a couple of selfish kids playing house.*

****

By the time Monday rolled around, I was juggling guilt, grief, and confusion better than a damn circus clown. *And about that text Friday night?* Yeah, Goldie never responded, her silence a curveball I hadn't seen coming. So, I messaged her this morning about meeting for lunch.

Radio. Fucking. Silence.

After Sofia left for lunch that day and again on Tuesday, I hurled frustration into the juggling act. Goldie had either tired of hanging out here, or she'd tired of being anywhere near me. My gut instinct leaned toward the latter.

On Wednesday, I resorted to swearing under my breath, feeling like a chewed-up wad of bubble gum that'd lost its flavor—that Goldie had stuck under her chair and forgotten. I'd replayed all the intimate moments from last week in my head so many times I thought it would explode.

Elbow on the desk and my palm cupping my cheek, I spun a highlighter around like a roulette wheel. *I don't want a one-night stand.* My words echoed in my mind. *If you don't feel the same, it might be best—for professional reasons, if nothing else—we stop while we still can.* I slammed my hand over the highlighter.

Suffering from sleep-deprivation, my patience was dangling on a very thin string when Bedrock—*Jeez, I've got to quit calling James that*—stopped at my desk. If it weren't for the spicy aroma lifting from the paper bag he dropped on my desk, I'd have steered him away. Hoping he missed my stomach's snarling, I shoved the highlighter aside and peeked underneath the bag, a faint line of greasy goodness now etched on my expense report from the Shembery trip.

"I got us Reubens from the corner deli—even had them add extra corned beef to yours." James dragged a chair to my desk and rolled up his sleeves. "No sauerkraut for you, though. You're sour enough already."

"Ha. Ha." I deadpanned.

By nature, James was a nester, a real fixer-upper kind of guy. In high school, after tinkering under the hood of his muscle car, teenage James liked to nestle with one of his girlfriends on the bunk in the back of the family garage. Adult James still liked to nest and snuggle, but only with Annabel now in the house they'd remodeled and—*dare I say it*—turned into a real home.

That's why James dropping by with one of my favorite lunches didn't surprise me. It was just the way my kid brother rolled…and one of the top reasons I knew he'd make a kick-ass father.

I unfolded the wrapper around my sandwich, pulled out the toothpick with the frilly blue cellophane top, and grabbed the garlic pickle spear. I crunched into it. "So, how's Annabel today?"

"Anna? Oh, she's awesome. Great," James mumbled over a mouthful of sandwich.

I drew down my brows. "Got to say the whole bedrest thing surprised me. I thought she was having a textbook pregnancy."

James nodded, licking a drop of Thousand Island dressing from the corner of his mouth. "Yeah. We're taking an abundance of caution. Never can be too safe, you know. Precious cargo and all."

Whenever my brother spoke in clichés, he was dodging something. I rubbed my tongue along the inside of my cheek. "Glad you got to stick around here last week." I took what remained of my pickle spear and pointed it in his direction. "Good to be all *cautious*. With Anna…and your *precious cargo*."

James dropped his sandwich and reached for a napkin, dragging it over his chin. "What the fuck, Max."

"Don't 'what the fuck' me," I said, polishing off my pickle. "I don't know what the hell you and Dad are doing, chaining me to the Shembery account, but leave me out of it."

"Remember Ethan? Appendicitis? A talented but inexperienced female engineer needing support?" James huffed. "God, you're one uptight asshole."

"Yeah? Well, I was the one out there last week picking up the slack for this company while you stayed here all cozied-up with your wife." I gazed into my sandwich like it was some kind of crystal ball, biting back a curse. "I've got a reason to be uptight."

"This has nothing to do with work. You kicked butt, as always."

We both laid into our sandwiches, chewing silently.

Finally, James uncapped his soda and took a swallow. "You're just pissed off you screwed things up with Goldie."

I jerked my head in his direction.

"You heard me."

I felt like we were in a standoff from some B-rate cop movie. *Except James is too damn nice to be a cop.* But I decided to play along anyway.

"And what makes you think there was something to screw up with Goldie?" I sank my teeth into the layers of warm corned beef—missing the sauerkraut, by the way—and waited while James tugged on his soda. He'd always struggled with digestion issues, but then inhaled his food like a ravenous mutt. As he raised his hand to muffle a belch, I raised an eyebrow. *I sure as hell hope Bedrock doesn't erupt right here on my desk.*

Recovering, James leaned forward on both elbows. "What I know comes straight from George, who got it from Sofia, who dragged it out of Goldie on Saturday night. George came over on Sunday to help me with the timing belts on the convertible, which is when he spilled the beans. To me. That you just weren't that into her."

Christ, we really were in a B-rate cop movie. *Or worse, a sappy rom-com.*

I rolled my chair over to the mini fridge, grabbed a bottle of water, and rolled back. "You know Sofia. God knows what she told George." I took a long drink, buying my time. "To screw something up would imply Goldie and I have a relationship outside of work." *Which I stupidly believed—especially after the amazing night we spent together. But clearly I'm spent bubblegum.*

"You could if you wanted to. Goldie's hot. And single. And you're—"

I cut him off with a glare.

"—er, slow-cooker warm and single."

I scoffed at the sheer truth of his description, then went for another bite of my sandwich.

"Damn it, Max. Get off your high horse and admit it. You like Goldie Vreeland."

"Even if I was interested, I don't think she feels the same way. About me." I tossed an unopened bag of potato chips in his direction. "Now eat these and shut up."

James snorted, diving into the chips. "Dude, what are you talking about?"

"Look, we're too old to swap stories about girls. Not that we ever did." Having only been with Ashley, I could sum up my romantic escapades in a hundred characters or less. James could write a damn novel.

My brother shot me a fair enough scowl, then added, "I've seen the way you look at her. Hell, I was the one pushing for you to go in place of Ethan, okay? Not Dad. Mom and I thought it'd be good for you. That *Goldie* would be good for you."

Jesus Christ. If I thought my family fixated on me in the treading-water stage of my marriage, they'd been off the chains since the split. Mom and James, being the fuzzy-hearted meddlers in the family, were insufferable. Thank God Jess had been abroad this past year, missing most of the fallout. Dad was the only one who'd given me space. *You gave it your best shot, Son.* His words had me circling back to Jack's comment. *Is* that *truly my problem? Feeling like a failure…?*

"And don't try to tell me you haven't noticed how Goldie lights up when you walk in the room." James' accusation pulled me back to the conversation.

"I wouldn't say she lights up," I said, emphasizing the last two words.

"What would you call it then?"

I shrugged one shoulder. "She maybe smiles at me a little too much."

"Ahh, that's her beauty pageant background. She slips into her glamor grin when she gets anxious or nervous." James shoved the last of his sandwich into his mouth and began chewing. Moments later, he said around the mouthful, "Wait. You didn't know?"

I let my frown speak for me.

James swallowed his food and lowered his tone. "Noted. So," he said, dragging out the syllable, "how about we change the subject? You know we missed you at Sunday dinner."

I muttered something nondescript, still trying to wrap my head around how James knew something this personal about Goldie, and I didn't. I thought I'd been an attentive listener, asking all the right questions. *I told her I wanted to know everything about her...*

"Did you hear Jess will be back home by Memorial Day?"

I made an ambivalent grunting noise, not even caring how my brother might interpret it, and slid further into my thoughts. Had I been so deep in my rebound glasses, so focused on our physical attraction, I'd missed the important stuff? She'd told me some things about the competitions, but nothing about worries or nerves...or smiles to hide them.

Fuck...an ever-loving...duck.

The vision of the lovely grinning parakeet sitting beside me on the plane ride home resurfaced in my brain. Ever since leaving Goldie in bed that morning, things had gone to shit. Had what we'd done made her nervous? Did I do something to make her anxious about coming back home? I groaned under my breath. Maybe Ash nailed it when she'd dubbed me the emotional equivalent of a rubber mallet.

"Guess what else? We changed our minds and asked the doctor to tell us what we're having. Yeah, it's a baby orangutan. Long arms, reddish hair—except on its butt."

The word snapped me out of my head. *A reddish haired,* "Orangutan?"

"Finally," James said, barking out a laugh. "I had to say *something* to get your attention."

I dropped my sandwich, shaking my head. "Sorry, man. I'm shitty company, and I know you're only trying to help. I've just got a lot on my mind."

James shifted in his chair. "I'm sorry about MerryBelle." Reading the question in my gaze, he added, "Ashley. She came by to see Anna and told her what happened."

I nodded a couple times. After having been tied up with my ex-wife all weekend, and never getting the chance to tell Goldie what happened, the need to talk about Merry pushed against my chest. I turned in my chair to face James, unloading my emotions like pellets from a pop gun.

"She was sick, James. And we didn't even know." I pulled down the last swallow of water, wiping my mouth with my sleeve. "I was clueless when Ashley called me at the ass-crack of dawn on Friday."

"That was it, you know."

My mouth opened and closed, then I flung the empty water bottle in the recycling bin.

James crumpled his sandwich wrapper and chip bag, shoving them in the paper sack. He looked me square in the eyes. "Goldie heard you on the phone with Ashley that morning."

Guess he knew she spent the night with me. *Whatever.* "No, she didn't. She was asleep."

"Dude. She was awake. She overheard you in the bathroom talking to your ex-wife."

My mind ticked through the bits and pieces of the phone call. "What the hell? I hardly remember anything I said."

"Well, Goldie sure does. Whatever you said made her think you were with Ashley. Like *with* with her. At least that's what Sofia told George she said. And George told me." James cocked his head. "It's bullshit, right? Tell me there's no way in hell you still have feelings for your ex-wife."

My head was swimming with the barrage of 'he said-she said.' I began folding the wrapper around what remained of my Reuben. "It's complicated, James."

"What the fuck does that mean?"

I pushed off my chair and glared at him. "What that means, Bedrock, is of course I care about Ashley. We were married for nine fucking years!" I jerked my head away, coughing back a laugh. "First, I ditch her at her tenure thing to take care of work. Then, she calls me—all sobbing and shit—saying MerryBelle's dead. While I was away. And I hadn't seen my dog in three weeks...and I didn't even get to say goodbye."

James started to speak, but I raised my hand. "I know it's not the same, nowhere close to having a child. But Merry belonged to us. And we loved her and losing her this way?" A lump the size of Alaska lodged in the back of my throat. "It hurts like hell."

James lowered his head, and for a moment he looked like the kid brother who left something of mine behind in our backyard fort when the ice cream truck came rolling through the neighborhood. *Something he shouldn't have had in the first place*. After stuffing himself with a couple of fudge pops, James took off on his bike with his friends...and a monsoon of a thunderstorm descended later that afternoon. It flooded our fort and ruined everything inside.

Loss to an eight-year-old kid was his little brother sneaking off with his comic book collection and then forgetting about it when he ran off with his friends.

"I'm sorry, Max. I was trying to help move things along with you and Goldie, but I shouldn't have butted in."

Loss to a thirty-one-year-old man wasn't all that different, only I didn't want my brother's apology or pity. This time around, he didn't owe me anything.

I pushed out a slow breath, needing to not sound like such an asshole. "That's where you're wrong. I'm glad you showed up—and with my favorite lunch." James' mouth softened into a smile. "I don't think I realized how bad I needed to get out of my head. And I had no idea Goldie overheard me on the phone with Ashley. I was in shock, I guess. I don't even remember what I said." I threw my head back and groaned. "Well, at least now I know what the fuck's wrong."

"Yeah, I passed by her office yesterday, and she didn't even look up. Had her eyes glued to the wall, chewing the hell out of a pencil. Not at all like the Goldie we know and love."

I cupped my hands behind my neck. "I thought she was finished with me, James. Through. Like being with me once was one time too many."

He barked out a laugh. "You know, for someone so fucking smart, you're sometimes a complete idiot."

I paced the length of my office, swung my head outside the door, and told Sofia to clear my afternoon. I turned to James. "Hey. Thanks. I owe you one."

"Eh, more like a dozen, but who's counting." He chuckled as he came to his feet, crossing his arms over his chest. "Now, how about you tell me what's with this *Bedrock* shit?"

I laughed, thankful for the levity in his voice, and cuffed him on the arm. "I'll explain later."

He cocked his head. "Because you've got more important things to do right now, yeah?"

"Yeah. I need to see a girl."

A grin reached his eyes. "I'll let you off the hook so long as you're going after the hot single engineer girl."

I scrubbed my hands over my face then gazed at my

brother. His eyes gleamed with warmth and understanding, and I wondered when he'd gotten so wise. Here I thought I was the one with the strong brotherly shoulders. *I stand corrected.*

"Christ, James. This is so messed up."

"Yeah. Your shit usually is. But I'm used to it," he said with a wink.

I affectionately flipped him the finger, grabbed my jacket, and skidded out the door.

Chapter Fifteen

Wednesday, May 19th 4:05 p.m.
Goldie
I slapped my hands on the water. *Enough with the drama already.* I needed to follow the advice I gave my Guppies. "Take off those floaters, suck it up, and start swimming." Except with five-year-olds, I left out the 'suck it up' part.

A sweet little lady wearing a vintage swim cap with white rubber daisies smiled at me from the edge of the pool. I mouthed an apology and swung out of the pool.

My gaze lifted to the large digital clock hanging on the wall. School had dismissed, and the swim team would be cutting up the lanes in a few minutes. I padded over to my chair, wrapped a towel around my body, and reached for my phone. My shoulders sank over the blank screen staring back at me. *I guess it's official. He's ghosting me back.*

I clutched my phone beneath my chin. Ever since I left Max hanging after a text on Friday night and another one on Monday morning, I'd been trying to convince myself I wanted his silence. It was best this way. He could reconnect all the dots he wanted with Ashley, relive all the moments he apparently missed with her, and I could move on. I *would* move on.

I blinked several times and rubbed my palm up my nose. I wished I could blame the stinging behind my eyes on the chlorine in the pool. I groaned inwardly, sliding into my flip-flops and slinging my backpack onto my shoulder. I turned, slamming into the six-foot-three frame of nicely dressed man.

Max lifted his hands, palms open, veering back in his stance. "Collide much, Ms. Vreeland?" One side of his mouth curved into a smile of mildly cocky...determination?

Well. Two can play that game.

Max's mouth twisted. "And please don't. I never want to see *that* smile again. At least not directed at me."

It took a few seconds for me to realize he wasn't joking. As my smile dissolved on my lips, I was fairly certain a curl of steam was circling around my ears. I'd spent hours at my orthodontist's office perfecting *that* smile, snapping hundreds of photos of myself until I committed the right one to muscle memory. It wowed the judges and at times, provided the perfect screen for my frazzled nerves.

Not at all certain I cared for his opinion, I planted my hands on my hips. "Dictate much, Mr. Corda?"

Some measure of frustration must have seeped into my expression because he tilted his head back and laughed. *Actually laughed.*

"Glad you find me amusing. Now, if you'll excuse me." I brushed past him, and he grabbed hold of my hand. His fingers flexed around my palm. *Dear Lord, I've missed your touch.*

"I'm not laughing at you. I'm laughing at me." He met my bewildered gaze. "I thought you didn't care anymore—about me or us. But thankfully, your little bit of spitfire there tells me what I need to know. Now," he said, stepping closer, "we need to talk."

In the time it took for Max to grab my other hand, I felt my real Goldie smile tugging at my lips. I didn't understand the power he had over me, how the combination of his mossy green eyes and mellow voice could blur my memory of his phone conversation with *her* so easily.

He lifted his chin, undeterred. "Tell me what you're thinking. Please…"

"How do you do it?"

He crinkled his brow. "Do what, Peach?"

"That," I clipped. "Right there." I tried to twist out of his grip, but it was pointless. I averted my gaze, hating my weakness. "You derail me with one look…and sweet talk."

"That's nothing. Just being near you makes me jump clear off the tracks."

I glanced at where his hands still held mine, and he slowly released them. I hitched my backpack higher on my shoulder, practically hugging it. My gaze flitted over his pressed charcoal slacks and polished shoes. *Italian leather is not pool-approved footwear.* A light sheen of moisture had formed on his dress shirt, and his tie begged to be loosened.

My fingers tightened around my shoulder strap. "You do know you're the only person here in dress clothes."

"What about him?"

I followed the direction of Max's gaze. "Pool chemical sales reps don't count."

"Better not let him hear you say that." He winked.

I pulled a full-on face of bewilderment. Max had been on auto replay in my head for days, and now he stood a foot away—in clothes I desperately wanted to rip

127

from his body—debating the merits of proper poolside attire and business protocol. The oddity of the situation begged a question.

"How did you find me anyway?" I raised my eyebrow. "Did Sofia tell—"

"No. She didn't." As the swim coach blew his whistle, Max took my elbow and steered us away from the oncoming traffic of kids. "When I saw your car wasn't in the parking lot, I called to find out the class schedule."

"Huh." I said, then added, "Stalk much?"

"Only since meeting you." Max straightened, squaring his shoulders. "And I don't like it."

I lifted my chin. "I like it."

"No, you don't." He closed the space between us, pure attraction thrumming between us. "Wouldn't you rather us be together in each other's lives and not sneaking around to peek at them?"

Of course, but—

"Again, we need to talk, Goldie." He pinned me with the weight of his gaze. "And not here."

I sighed at the wisdom in his words but still felt like a dingy floating in the Indian Ocean. *You know, in that area where airplanes crash and are never seen again?* My pulse skittered, and as if sensing it, he took my hand, rubbing his thumb over my wrist. Even when in danger of capsizing in the scariest ocean on the planet, somehow I knew Max would save me.

If I let him. I stole a glance at him, biting my lower lip. "Wanna grab a smoothie?"

"No."

"A sandwich?"

Max chuckled. "Food is part of the plan, yes. I was

thinking you could take a shower at my place while I make supper."

His place? My toes curled inside my flip-flops. *Slap, he cooks, too?*

"Please, Goldie?"

In the end, the tremor in his voice undid me. My gaze softened, and shifting my weight to one side, I lifted my chin. "You had me at 'collide.' "

He feathered his hand through his hair, the rogue curl falling across his brow. "You know you stole that line from a movie, right?"

"I do, and it's one of my favorites."

Another blast came from the coach's whistle followed by the splash of bodies diving into the water, and my heart tightened. *Or maybe it's my DEFCON One triggering my cardiac arrest.*

"We should watch it sometime." Max went for my hand and squeezed it gently.

"You like romantic comedies?"

"No, but I like you." He raised my hand to his lips and kissed my knuckles. "And only you."

He added that last part as if he knew how badly I needed to hear it. My feelings had been a merry-go-round for days, and I was just so tired of thinking about him, the phone call, and all the things I'd left unsaid. He said we needed to talk. Thank God, because I was ready to listen.

The tingle his lips left on my knuckles emboldened me. "Can we snuggle together on the sofa while we watch it?"

"Yeah, with a couple of cold beers and a bowl of lightly salted popcorn."

I loved how Max encouraged my healthy eating, but

tonight I wanted to indulge. "Could we go all out and get the loaded butter kind?"

He offered me his arm, and I accepted it. "I think that can be arranged, Peach."

Chapter Sixteen

Wednesday, May 19th 5:20 p.m.
Max

Dressed in the swimsuit and shorts she'd worn from the fitness center, Goldie followed me to my bedroom. I offered her my favorite college sweatshirt and a pair of my socks, and as she clutched my things to her chest, two spots rose to color her cheeks. When she disappeared into my bathroom, I grinned, wondering how the shirt would look on her. Baggy? *Absolutely*. Sexy? *Hell, yes*. There was something intimate about a woman wearing her man's clothes. Of course, I was assuming she wanted me to be her man. Once I heard the shower door close, I stepped into my closet and changed into a Henley shirt and black running pants.

Downstairs, I prepped the vegetables—mushrooms, baby spinach, garlic, and shallots—and dumped them into the cast-iron skillet, swirling them in a bit of olive oil. I could hear the running water and chuckled as Goldie launched into the chorus of a Broadway tune. *She's not kidding when she says singing isn't her talent.* Somehow knowing she wasn't perfect released some of the tension in my shoulder muscles.

I stirred the vegetables in the pan, the nuttiness of the garlic wafting to my nose, then took the skillet off the gas. With voice command, I chose a playlist—not *the* playlist...not yet anyway—then lifted the lid on the risotto and added the vegetables. I heard the shower cut off and gazed at the clock. Just enough time for that to simmer while I seasoned the scallops.

When Goldie came strolling into the kitchen with my sweatshirt skimming her thighs—and my imagination drifted to what color panties were hidden underneath—the temperature in the room spiked. The vision of her bare legs caught my breath, and the way the heels of my socks reached up past hers made me grin. I liked how she'd twisted her hair into a messy bun, the loose-fitting neckline of my sweatshirt baring the curve of her shoulder. I stilled, envisioning the perfect breasts I'd caressed a week ago rubbing against the soft fabric. *I may never wash it again.*

Goldie slid onto a barstool at the island and folded her arms on the granite countertop, getting the bird's-eye view of the stove. "A girl could get lost upstairs. Too bad I ate my raisins before swim class. I could've used them to leave a trail around your master suite."

I laughed, drizzling more olive oil in the skillet before tossing in the scallops. The sizzle in the pan matched the energy in the room. "Trust me. There's no way I'm letting you get lost…in my house or anywhere else." I glanced over in time to catch her squinting at a scuff on my cabinet.

"Do you have any cinnamon?"

"Uh, sure. Pantry's over there," I said with a flick of my head. My gaze followed her as she walked across the kitchen and back.

Goldie held the bottle in her hand. "Do you even know how powerful cinnamon is?"

I shook my head, stirring the scallops while she sprinkled some cinnamon into her palm. When she licked her pinky finger and dipped it in the powder, rubbing it over the mark, I did a double take.

"See there?" She pulled back, tilting her head. "The scuff's all gone." She stepped over to the sink and rinsed her hands under the faucet. "The Egyptians used cinnamon as an embalming agent. It repairs broken hair follicles and repels moths, too. I've used cinnamon sticks to soothe Athlete's Foot, which is a real thing even when you wear shower shoes at a place as clean as the fitness center."

"And don't forget cinnamon rice cakes," I added, loving how her grin reached her eyes. "Sounds like it's the Eighth Wonder of the World."

She laughed, and the sound bubbling from her lips did something funny in my chest. Undeterred, she walked her fingers over the vegetables my housekeeper had left in a bowl on the counter. "And then, I fell into an Internet rabbit hole the other night and landed on an article, 'Fifty Ways to Use Avocados.'"

"Only fifty?"

She giggled. "Yeah, kind of a stretch really. Only about half of them were actually *good* ideas." Goldie reached for an avocado, adding, "We could grill one to go with supper, if you'd like."

I turned to face her, noticing how her expression shifted like the colors in a mood ring. From bronze when she was tackling something new to soft pink when she was game-ready.

I turned on the gas to the grill side of the stove top. "Sounds perfect."

We got busy with our meal prep, brushing elbows and sharing stories. At one point, my gaze drifted to her hands. She gripped my chef's knife like an old friend, cutting into the avocado and drizzling each half with olive oil, salt, and pepper. I nudged the ceramic utensil jar toward her, and she grabbed the tongs, flashing me a thank you smile.

When all the food came together, I glanced over my shoulder. "How about you pour the wine while I get this on our plates?" As she padded across my kitchen floor, the sight of her—the straight line of her back and gently curved hips—convinced me she belonged here. *Now to convince you.*

I'd been playing out in my head how this would go. Goldie with me in my home, in my bed. Making love to her all night long.

But that was before I botched things up.

And Goldie had withdrawn into herself.

I shook my head, pushing back the last thought and walking toward her. The wine gurgled as she poured it in the glasses, and I put the plates on the table. "First, we eat." I held out the chair for her and raised my glass, our gazes meeting. "Then, we talk."

****

As sunset faded into night, Goldie snuggled with me on the sofa while I spilled my guts about the phone call with Ashley. Though the loss of Merry felt like shrapnel wedged in my heart, Goldie lessened the sting. She wrapped her arms around my waist, pressing her cheek against my chest. As her breathing fell in sync with mine, I relaxed my shoulders and drew her closer.

"Oh, my God, Max." Regret etched Goldie's voice. "I-I'm sorry. What a terrible shock. You must miss her so much."

"It's not really hit me yet. I still have her pet bed and chew toys. I tried, but I couldn't get rid of them. Not yet anyway."

She tilted her head, tucking her forehead under my chin. "I don't know what came over me, why I assumed the worst."

I sighed. "It's okay. I don't even remember what I said to Ashley on the phone. All I remember was feeling cold and numb, wanting to drown in a hot shower and climb back in bed with you."

"But I'd left…"

"Yeah." I pressed my lips to the strands of hair alongside her temple. "But only after you thought I'd left you."

We were silent for some time, breathing in unison. Sometimes silence felt uncomfortable, rising like a dough, tripling in size and covering every inch of space in the bowl. But this silence wasn't suffocating. It felt like the space we needed to find our way back to each other.

"I wish I'd stayed, Max. Faced my fear."

I shifted her in my arms, studying the spray of tiny freckles on her cheeks and the delicate arch of her eyebrows. The corners of her eyes softened under my gaze, and my protective instincts awakened. She'd given me patience, and I owed her the same.

"I never want you to feel afraid with me. I wish you'd told me what you heard, but I can only imagine how much it hurt. I'd give anything to undo the pain." I kissed her forehead. "You were probably wondering why I'd take Ashley's call in the first place."

"Yeah." The word fell heavy from her lips.

"It was part habit, I guess. She calls, I answer. But honestly? I knew something was up for her to call at that hour." I tilted her chin toward me. "But I should've stayed with you—let you hear everything because there was nothing to hide." I sighed and lowered my hand. "I don't know why I didn't."

Goldie took my fingers and brought them to her lips, kissing them. "Sounds like we both did things we don't fully understand."

As she settled into my arms again, my fingers toyed with her hair and my mind ticked through a flurry of thoughts, landing on the book Andy had given me—that I'd finished Sunday night. *True intimacy is earned, not given.*

I carefully formed the words I needed to say in my head before setting them free. "I see a counselor, Goldie." I waited, and her nod encouraged me. "His name is Andy Howell, and I've been seeing him every Wednesday for close to two years. He's helping me work through a lot of issues, and not just ones about the divorce."

She placed her palms on my shoulders and gently pushed back. "That's good. We're all working on something."

"Intimacy." I whooshed out a breath, lowering my gaze. "I'm working on intimacy. I want to let others into my life—especially you. It's just hard for me."

She tugged my chin toward her. "Mine is adequacy. Sometimes I'm afraid I'm not enough."

While her statement struck me as nothing short of ridiculous, I understood something about the need to be heard. I met her gaze. "That phone call didn't help, huh?"

She shook her head.

"I'm sorry," I said, cramming every ounce of feeling into those two words. I closed my mouth and waited to hear what she needed.

She shifted, drawing her knees up and wrapping her arms around them. "I was eighteen before I had my first kiss. I would've loved to be Ashley, having the security of a boyfriend like you." She shrugged one shoulder. "I had lots of friends, but I don't know why boys never liked me like that. Maybe it was the pageants or band or being such a math geek, who knows."

The way she was curled into a ball reminded me of a kitten stuck in a tree, but I resisted the urge to wrap her in my protective embrace. *That's what I want, not what she needs.*

Even with a steady girlfriend, I'd experienced some teenage insecurities, so I leaned into those feelings. "I'm sure that was hard. Boys are pretty shallow at that age. My guess is they were intimidated."

"That's what Ace said." She bit her lower lip before continuing. "I was fifteen when I entered my first competition—the Miss Labor Day pageant—on a dare. I didn't have to win or anything, just have the guts to enter. I figured I didn't have a chance, but when I got to the final three, I was stunned. I found out later from Kyle Peterson only my talent got me to the final round."

"What the hell did he know about it?"

"His dad was our mayor and a contest judge, and Kyle said he overheard him talking about it."

"So, you play a mean trumpet, Ms. Vreeland?"

"Nope. I played my grandmother's dulcimer."

I raised my eyebrows. "Now that's pretty cool."

"I know, right?" She raised up, chin lifted. "I'd go see her on Sunday afternoons, and she taught me every song she knew. After that, I played the dulcimer in every contest I entered and threw every win in Kyle's face."

"Sounds to me like there was something more to this

guy than you're telling me."

Several silent beats passed between us while she collected her emotions…and I put mine in check. My hands fisted the blanket around us.

"So…we were playing Spin the Bottle at this boy-girl party in sixth grade. Kyle thought his spin would land on the cute soccer player girl beside me, and when it didn't, he stared at me like I was a pig wearing lipstick."

"I want to flatten this kid's face."

"I did, too. He came in for the kiss, but he turned his head at the last second, and all I got was his cheek. I played it cool, laughing about it with my friends, but his rejection hurt." She searched my face then shrugged. "And that was it for me and boys. I never had a date, or a real kiss, until I went to college. And even then, the two guys I dated were pretty much jerks."

I cupped her cheeks with my palms. "Well, you've found the right partner now. At least, I hope you feel that way."

"I do. And I'll never not trust you again, Max. Not ever."

****

Goldie

I settled back into Max's arms, the scent of his clean sandalwood soap teasing my nose and stripping away what seemed like the zillion hours we'd been apart. I hated how I'd cut and run the last time we were together. I didn't want to be the girl who shied away anymore. With Max by my side, I felt I was learning how to build a fire, not just strike a match.

I. Am. Enough.

And Max is an abundance, I mused, tracing my

finger over the lines in his palm.

My brain began circling back to the little things I noticed about him last week, like how he held his pen in a tripod grip, drank his coffee black, and fiddled with something in his pants pocket—coin change, most likely—when he was restless. The image of the white tank undershirts he'd worn when we video-talked popped into my head, and I blinked, wondering if he used fabric softener or dryer sheets in his laundry, and whether he rolled or crumpled his toothpaste tube. *Does he recycle…?*

I turned inside the circle of his arms, my thoughts drifting back to his candlelit hotel room and the sound of waves lapping the beach. I caught my lip between my teeth. *I remember the small brown birthmark on your shoulder and long second toes that are so damn sexy.*

"I'm going to learn what that look of yours means if it's the last thing I do." Max dragged the throw blanket at our feet around me like a cape.

"If you do, I'm done for. I'll never be able to look at you with a straight face again."

He bent and brushed his lips over my earlobe. "Straight faces are highly overrated."

I toyed with the button on his Henley shirt. "I'll tell you what's behind mine if you tell me what's behind yours—your serious look, I mean."

"Deal. But you go first."

"I was daydreaming…about you."

"Anything special?"

"Just thinking about how you hold your pen with a tripod grip and take your coffee black. Do you recycle?"

Max coughed a laugh, then hugged me closer. "As a matter of fact, I do. I also sanitize my expresso machine on the fifteenth of the month and change the air conditioning filters on the thirtieth." I hid a giggle behind my hand. "Sorry, but my ego is a little bruised, Peach."

"I might have also been thinking about your sexy toes and this," I said, sliding his neckline over to expose his birthmark. I rubbed my finger over it.

"I like how you catalog things, squirreling them away in your beautiful mind."

Oh, you don't know the half of it. I laid my head against his chest so I could hear the thrum of his heart. "Now, it's your turn. Tell me about your serious look."

"Well, according to my mother, it's her fault I was fourteen going on forty. Something about relying on me too much to look after my siblings. But she's wrong. It's just how I'm wired. I look before I leap. I protect my place in line. I make sure everyone's buckled in and check to be sure the doors are locked." He tightened his hold on my hips, squeezing them for emphasis. "And just so you know, I hate sharing."

"I love you." *Holy crap.* Panic crawled into my throat, and I prayed I hadn't really strung those three words together. *Out loud.* But I blurted it into his chest, right? *Maybe he didn't hear me?*

He rubbed his hands over my arms. "You know, I have some pretty deep feelings about you, too."

Seconds ticked by while I tossed around the weight of his response to my not-so-little bombshell. Deep down, I felt there was nothing wrong with giving voice to honest feelings, but I absolutely didn't want Max worrying—after all our confessions tonight—I was some obsessed, clingy, love-struck juvenile. My hand lingered on the buttons of his Henley shirt, and I rubbed my thumb over the smooth threads in the top one. As I tilted my head upward, my nose brushed his throat. "Oh, please…like I don't even know where that came from, like what I meant to say was…well, of course, I love that *part* of you—the caring and protective part—and I do truly love it…very much."

"I didn't know one sentence could be so long. Did you even remember to breathe?" Max asked with a soft chuckle.

I understood his attempt to lighten the mood, but I play-swatted his bicep anyway. "You can get the popcorn and beer anytime now. I'm sure that movie's streaming on one of your services."

"You had me at 'sexy toes.' "

I buried deeper into his embrace. "Oh, really? And not 'I love you?' "

"Hey," he said, tightening his arm around me. "Would you feel better if I told you I wished I could be so free with my feelings?"

I shook my head against his chest, and feeling the warmth of his gaze on the top of my head, I envisioned forest green eyes hiding behind dark lashes. "Wishing's not the same as trying."

"Ahh." Max stretched out the syllable, cupping his arms at my back. "A dare, is it?"

I nodded, my nose brushing the chest hair peeking out from beneath his shirt. The sensation interfered with my breathing, but it didn't matter because he suddenly pushed me back.

Max ran his finger along the curve of my jaw. "I need you to be patient with me, okay?" When I opened my mouth, he pressed his finger to my lips. "Please listen."

I swallowed hard, relenting to the pull of his voice.

"I'm not an easy man, Goldie. And I'm especially not easy to love." He dragged his hand around the back of his neck, sighing. "I've already told you about the intimacy thing, but I'm also working on my issues of falling short on the big things in life. I need to learn something from my failed marriage. Right now, I'm not sure what that is, but I know I can't figure it out alone." He looked away, the curl of hair I loved falling over his brow, then added, "I'm pretty much a mess."

I waited a respectful number of seconds, then placed my palm on his cheek. "Mess is best, remember?" I grinned when his eyes sparkled with recognition. "Yours, mine, and ours." My thumb drifted over to the corner of his mouth tilted in a smile. "We're partners, so maybe if we try—and with a little bit of luck—we'll figure out the mess together."

Max slowly pulled me into a kiss, his tongue stroking possessively against mine. The pressure left me dizzy, holding on to his shoulders when he leaned back. "We have to be honest with each other, Goldie. From now on no more assumptions, no more retreating behind that *smile* and the parrot chatter."

I'd give him what he asked for and then some. *But please be gentle with me.* My heartbeat hammered away in my chest. "I-I won't. I'll tell you if something's on my mind. Promise."

He lowered his face and pressed his forehead to mine. "I've never wanted a woman the way I want you. I want to make love to you. Christ, I'm borderline obsessed with you."

Now there's something I can absolutely relate to. As his hands slid lower and cupped my ass, I wiggled against the ridge forming inside his pants. "Are you making a pass at me, Max?"

He nipped at my jawline. "Nah."

"Oh, you're definitely hitting on me."

"No way, Peach," he said, lips sucking on my earlobe.

"Well, then it's something close to it."

"Oh, no. Not by a longshot." He lowered his voice to a gravelly whisper. "I'm fucking crushing on you."

I had no words for a comeback. I didn't need any. I only needed Max.

Chapter Seventeen

Wednesday, May 19th 9:30 p.m.
Max
I lifted Goldie's chin and kissed her tenderly, a spring-breeze kind of kiss laced with the starlight I saw reflected in her blue eyes. I moved my lips across hers with a duality of sexuality and patience…like we could do nothing but kiss for the next few hours and that would be enough. I drew her lower lip between mine, sucking softly. When an airy gasp escaped her mouth, I pulled her closer, squeezing her perfect ass.

"Your kisses are the sweetest things," I said against her lips, trying to steal her breath. "I want to learn every dip, every point and curve of your body with my mouth."

As Goldie's head fell backward, I gazed at the swell of her breasts above the loose neckline of my sweatshirt. Her boobs were pin-up perfect, an image even the drought of the past week couldn't diminish. I slid my hands underneath the sweatshirt and unhooked her bra. I cupped one mound, thumbing her nipple to a tight point, all the while marking her neck with soft kisses.

When the sound of rolling water jets cut through the quiet hum of our kissing, Goldie flinched. I flicked my head toward the patio. "Hot tub. I set the timer before supper."

"Confident much?"

"Nah, mostly hopeful." I touched a curl that'd fallen

free from her bun. "Will you join me?"

Goldie pushed off me and stepped back, a blush rising in her cheeks. She pulled off the sweatshirt and bra, dropping them on the floor.

Damn, she's so beautiful and curvy. I stood, dragging my shirt over my head, and tossing it aside.

"Wait." I closed the space between us, peeling off her cotton panties and my socks. I moved behind her, studying her bun before loosening the wrap holding it in place. Her thick hair fell into my palms, and I brushed it over her shoulder. I kissed a path down her neck, wanting to mark her as mine. Without even trying, Goldie fired the urges I'd buried away years ago. I grew stiffer with thoughts of her, and I shed my remaining clothes.

Without words, I refilled our wineglasses and gave her a follow me motion with my head, leading her to the hot tub on the back porch. Of the four condos designed within Bladen House, mine was the largest and most secluded. While there was adequate foliage and fencing around the property, I had a privacy shield installed along with the hot tub last year for added assurance.

I lifted the lid on the patio bench and pulled out a pair of thick spa towels. I placed them by the tub and turned to her. "You know I think preparedness—"

"Is a virtue," Goldie chimed in.

I chuckled under my breath, as though standing naked with her, making no effort to hide my arousal, was as natural as the breeze stirring the windchimes. I held her hand while she stepped in the hot tub, and I watched her body disappear beneath the bubbles. After selecting an instrumental playlist, I joined her in the water. I stared as she knotted her hair in a bun without any tie.

"Kind of cool, huh?" Goldie tilted her head, tucking

a wisp behind her ear.

I reached for her, lacing our fingers together. "I love your long hair, and if that makes me a caveman, I apologize."

"When I was little, I got teased for being a tomboy." She slid deeper in the water, submerging her shoulders, and released a languid sigh. "I started growing my hair out in fifth grade when I still wore an A cup bra. Had no idea within a couple years my boobs would pretty much silence the whole gender thing."

"Kids say some stupid shit," I said, watching her lick a drop of wine from her lip and wishing I'd gotten to it first.

"Yeah, they really do. But my parents raised us to go out there and fix our problems, you know? Grab the bull by the horns and all that kind of stuff."

I stared at her from over the rim of my glass, the rippling water dancing a salsa over her bare shoulders and cleavage.

"I'm glad you like them." Goldie giggled, the sound steering me back to the conversation. "The girls are big," she said, lifting her breasts so the bubbles barely covered her nipples, "but right now, I'm pretty happy with them."

I slid closer, caressing her arm. I tried to school my expression, but that imagery had lassoed all coherent thought in my brain.

"You should be. I love your boobs." I cupped them in my hands, enjoying the soft hiss of her breath. "Do you know I've dreamed about them?" As she shook her lovely head, I grew even harder. "Do you have any idea how long I've dreamed of making love to you?"

Her cheeks pinked, and it had nothing to do with the steam in the hot tub. We could be in the frozen tundra, her hidden under a dozen layers of clothes, and she'd still fire my desire.

"Almost as long as I've wanted—"

You. Her word disappeared beneath my kiss, and I parted her lips with my tongue, needing to be closer to her. I wanted to be gentle, but her admission forced me into unchartered territory. My need to possess her, to show her how much I wanted to deserve her love, crowded out all other thoughts. I drew her closer, desperate to feel the friction of her skin against mine. She slid her knee between my legs, and in a split second, her thigh rubbed against my hard length. I spread out my hands, shaping her tush and stilling her hips, bringing her around to straddle me.

Goldie broke our kiss, rising on her knees and leaning into me, trickles of water rolling down her skin. *It's like you read my damn mind.* I pressed small soft kisses to the sensitive undersides of her breasts, then ran my tongue over the tight points of her nipples. I drew one into my mouth, pulling it between my lips, loving the fluttering gasp—a mix of surprise and pleasure—that passed her lips.

My pulse throbbed through my veins, and I wanted her with me. My thumb found her tight, sweet pearl, and I stroked it in rhythm with my lips on her breast. My chest swelled as I sensed her moving toward her pleasure. I moved one finger lower, tracing a circle around her entryway before slipping it inside. For a moment, I imagined being notched there, her spasming muscles pulling me inside. *Christ, you're so close.*

"Oh, God," she panted. "I'm almost—I'm so close."

I hid my snicker against her breast, and when her knees buckled, I held her, kissing her trembling body until she collapsed against me. She ran her fingers through my hair, tugging on the ends of it at the back of my neck.

Our gazes locked, and I knew Goldie was right there and the simplest thing in the world would be to slide into her. *But definitely not the safest.* Somehow I found a trace of willpower and moved, stepping out of the tub and grabbing our towels. I tied one around my waist, and after helping her out of the water, wrapped her in the other. I snaked my arms around her and held her close. *You really are my missing puzzle piece.*

I kissed the top of her head. "I'm going to make love to you all night long. I've never wanted anything more in my life."

She unwound her hair, and when she tilted her head back, I smoothed it behind her shoulders. She traced her finger over my bottom lip. "Well, in that case, you'll need to switch over to *our* playlist…and set it on repeat."

"My bossy, brainy, beautiful Peach. I like the way you think."

****

Goldie

Max held my hand, leading me through the kitchen and upstairs. From behind, I spotted the two sexy dimples above his ass and fisted my free hand to keep from touching them. He moved with quiet purpose, kicking the bedroom door closed behind him and wrapping his arms around my waist. My towel floated to the floor about the same time I yanked his from his hips. For several quiet seconds we stood together, barely a breath separating us.

"You okay?" Max brushed a damp strand of hair off my face. There was no pressure in his question, only consideration. The gesture reminded me of when I'd first sat beside him in the airplane, his hand on my headrest.

"We're doing this, aren't we?" I murmured, wishing I could pinch myself to be sure I wasn't dreaming. "We're like actually, really *really* doing this…"

"Only if it's what you want." His voice slipped into a thick, relaxed tone, melting my insides. "I could hold you in my arms, and it'd still be the best night of my life."

As moonlight washed over our bodies, I rubbed my palms over his chest, appreciating the contrast of his tan skin against mine. I traced my thumbs over his collarbone, then slid my hands around his neck. "You're amazing, and I love—" I clipped the word at the tip of my tongue.

"Don't hold back. I need to know what you're feeling."

"I love being with you. I want you. I-I'm just still trying to make sense of this."

"Me, too." Max squeezed my hips. "And by 'this,' I mean 'us.' "

He captured my gaze. Could he possibly understand the implications of that word? *Us.* Max might not know it, but I was already his.

I pushed away the breath separating us, needing his heat, molding my body to his. On tiptoes, I brushed my lips against his, and they touched…and teased…then tangled. He showered me in gentleness, one hand moving along my spine, the other caressing the curve of my waist. My breath came faster, the sensations converging inside me all at once.

Max carefully stepped me backward toward the bed, breaking our kiss only to pull back the duvet. I knee-walked on the king-size mattress, carving out a cozy space for us amongst the pillows. At the sound of foil ripping, I turned, dragging my gaze from the tight lines of his calves up to his broad chest, then lower to his ripped stomach and rock-hard length. Warm silky desire swooshed in my lower belly, along with a bit of trepidation.

"I-I think you might need to go easy with me. It's been awhile. And you're so—" I gulped some air around the words—*fucking big*—knotted in my throat. Judging by the smile tugging at his mouth, he'd heard the sound.

"I'm going to take care of you, Peach. I'm in no rush."

Max moved over me, sheltering me. *Loving me.* His kisses lingered at my earlobe, then inched their way along the slope of my neck. His fingers swept over my belly while his lips lingered over my breasts. My emotions swirled like a cyclone. When I trembled in his arms, he rained kisses on my skin, murmuring sweet words about my gorgeous hair and wanting the cloud of it spread out over his thighs.

Oh. Dear. Lord.

Then his honeyed voice turned almost reverent, praising my breasts and the smooth skin of my inner thighs. As Max began describing—with naughty words whispered against my skin—what my body did to him, I quivered on the verge of another release, moaning.

"God, I love how responsive you are. I think if I touch you here," Max said, circling his nose over my sensitized bud, "you'll be right at the edge…almost…there."

With one touch of his lips, I arched toward his mouth and let the rush of pleasure take me where he wanted me to go. A string of sensuous moments cradled us, and as the music lifted in the air, I reached for him, pulling him up my body.

We kissed, and I tasted me on his lips. "You do that *really* well." His wolfish smile stirred an ache in my core. "I want you, Max."

He raised up to his knees, took the condom, and rolled it on. He came back, covering me with his body but careful to bear the weight on his elbows. Our lips melted together, like our bodies would do in a few moments. He nudged between my folds, sliding back and forth with each flex of his hips.

He gazed at me, eyes liquid dark and simmering. "Jesus Christ. I can't believe how good you feel—how ready you are."

I felt him right there, teasing my entryway. I lifted my hips, drawing him inside me as he pushed forward. He repeated the movement, sliding through and stretching me.

"Fuck," he rasped, head down, chin touching his chest.

I wrapped my legs around his lower back, opening to his sweet thrusts. When he finally reached home, I gasped with the sensation of how deeply, how completely, he filled me.

He kissed my forehead. "Please tell me I didn't hurt you."

I cupped his jawline, rubbing my thumbs over his cheeks, amazed that in the realization of how *connected* we were, his thoughts were of me. I shook my head, adjusting to the fullness, squeezing him with my pelvic muscles.

"Jesus," he gasped on a push of air.

"I know, right?" I grinned, pulling him to me, kissing his Adam's apple.

"My *naughty*, bossy, brainy, beautiful Peach." He lifted my chin, lightly kissing me before adding, "Do it again."

"Is that a dare…?" I leaned my head back against the pillow and hugged my contraction around his length, reveling in how he grew thicker by the second.

"My God." His expression grew darker, warmer. "You're so tight."

Wanting to please Max more than take my next breath, I rolled my hips against his. "Please…make love to me."

As he smiled a kiss to my lips, a razor-edged groan reverberated in his chest. He moved inside me with slow, deep thrusts, in perfect rhythm with the music. The soulful melody filled the air, and I watched how he fixed his gaze to where we were joined. He pumped into me with such raw sensuality, my body arched to meet him.

Max lifted his head, speaking to me with his jungle green gaze and hard-set jawline. I glided my hands over his arms and shoulders, fingernails scoring the cords of his muscles. He hooked my leg higher on his hip, angling me so he rubbed against my tight nub, working me with incredible thrusts until I fell apart.

I cried out his name, my breath coming in skittering squeaks like air escaping a balloon, but my gaze never left his. I wanted to be with him while he chased his pleasure. He really started to move then, intense and urgent, fingers digging into my hips. When his cadence skipped and his hips jerked, I pulled him closer, loving how his growl of release vibrated over my skin. I felt full and complete, a trembling mass of emotion beneath his powerful body.

His breathing was heavy and ragged, and his scent, laden with perspiration, wafted to my nose. He lowered his face and pressed his forehead to mine. "Holy fuck. I've never come so hard in my life."

Long languid seconds passed by, and if he wasn't still buried inside me, I would've floated away, as weightless as a straw wrapper. And when I told him as much, he chuckled.

Max leaned in to kiss me then withdrew and moved to the edge of the bed. He removed the condom and dropped it in the wastebasket, then peered over his shoulder. "I'll be right back."

"Max?" Even I was shocked at the shrill of my voice.

He placed his hand on my thigh. "Just going to get you a warm washcloth."

"For…?"

He scooted around to face me. "I, well, I…thought you'd want to—you know…"

As this mental picture took shape, my heart clinched. *God, Ashley really is frigid cold.* I shook my head. "No. No, I don't." I pulled back the covers and plumped the pillow beside me. "Please…? I like being messy with you. I want to smell you on my skin."

After the crease faded from his brow, Max came to me, pulling me into his arms, and I threaded my legs between his. His heart drummed in his chest, and the sound lulled me into a place of bliss. He stroked my back while I snuggled against his chest.

"Goldie?"

"Hm?"

His chest expanded then fell on a deep breath.

"Don't leave, okay? Not tonight, not next week, or next month. Stay with me."

I rolled onto my elbow, gazing at his mussed hair. I smoothed it back then pressed a kiss to his forehead. From beneath my eyelashes, I glimpsed his rigid length pressed against his stomach. He gazed at me with a dark twinkle in his eyes, and I wrapped my palm around him.

"Wild horses couldn't drag me away, Max." I kissed his earlobe while sliding my hand along his length. "You'll have to push me out the door just to get me to the office." A trace of a smile curved his lips, and feeling emboldened, I moved lower. "But right now, I remember something about you wanting me spread over your thighs?"

"God, yes. Your beautiful hair—" He sucked in his breath when I brushed my nose over his length. "I can't seem to get enough of you, Goldie. Never…enough…"

I hummed my agreement, settling in and showering him with my unconditional love.

Chapter Eighteen

One Month Later
Wednesday, June 23rd 12:30 p.m.
Max
Free-falling was not something I considered a thrill.
If life—and being a pilot—had taught me anything, it
was how to maneuver its dips and turns to maintain
altitude. Though dating Goldie for the past month had
produced a strong headwind—making love with her in
every room in my house—our relationship was
exhilarating.

I raised my glass to my lips, taking a lengthy
swallow over that thought. At my last counseling
session, Andy had commended me for taking the
relationship leap but suggested I tackle the important
conversations this time around. *Don't be blindsided if
Goldie frowns at your gun cabinet when you failed to ask
her thoughts on legal gun ownership.* I took a bite of pot
roast and chewed thoughtfully. *And don't ask her to fly
away with you, Max. Ask her where she wants to go.*

Hearing a little cough, I looked up—fork in hand—
and met Ashley's gaze. And just like that, I was teetering
at the edge of a cliff...*free-falling.* My ex-wife stood
close enough for her rose and lily scent to punch me in
the gut.

As I lowered my fork to the plate and gestured to the
seat across from me, Ashley signaled the waitress and

ordered an iced tea. She hung her purse on the back of the chair and folded her hands on the tabletop, charm bracelet circling her left wrist. I knew the count of charms by heart, but my gaze drifted to one in particular. I snatched a napkin from the pop-up dispenser, dragged it over my mouth, and crumpled it in my hand.

Ashley smiled. "I thought I'd find you here. You always did love Thomason's Pot Roast Wednesday." She cast a sideways glance at an old guy in a nearby booth craning his neck in our direction, then turned her gaze to the white bag on the table. "Still taking a chocolate turnover back to the office for Sofia?" When the waitress brought her drink, she tore open the straw and uttered a quiet thank you.

"It's cherry today." Despite knowing that chewing and free-falling were never a good mix, I stuck my fork into a couple of carrots and shoveled them into my mouth. "So, what's up?"

She reached for her hair—the front piece dangling by her cheek—and looped it around her finger. I'd watched her do that since our first days in freshman Civics, twisting the tendril while our teacher clicked through a slideshow about the rule of law in a democracy. I smirked into my next mouthful of stew.

"Don't laugh at me." She glanced at her crooked finger and huffed, raising her glass. "You have annoying habits, too."

I gave her a perfunctory nod. "Too many to count, if memory recalls." When she didn't reply, I put down my fork. I reached for the glass of water sweating a ring on the laminate tabletop and brought it to my lips. *Yeah, she makes me sweat, too.* I swallowed, then lowered the glass, sighing. "I'm sorry, Ash. That was rude. Why don't you just tell me why you're here."

The light returned to her eyes, and she tilted her head toward me. "You absolutely won't believe it, Maxie. I have the most exciting news!" She all but squealed the words, and I arched my eyebrows. "I've arranged for us to meet with Greer Pennington to discuss the complete redesign at the University. The Board just approved it, and the bidding closes next month. Infrastructure, grounds, gardens—the long overdue renovation we've dreamed about would be a windfall for CDD."

I leaned forward on my elbows, my freefall momentarily suspended. "If you're screwing with me—"

"I would never do that." She clasped her hands around her glass of tea. "I know how important work is to you—the number of times we tried to pitch this in the past. But things have changed with the new administration. We'll have the ear of Vice-Chancellor Pennington tomorrow evening. And he's ready to listen."

"Greer…?" I scratched my head, a grin spreading across my face. "Well, I'll be damned. I-I need to tell Dad. He'll be—"

"No, Maxie," Ashley said, shaking her head. "Dr. Pennington only wants to meet with us."

I gazed at her, the smile tugging at the corners of her mouth rewinding time like the locking wheel inside a clock. She was forever paving the path forward, figuring out the next move for us. *Only there's no longer an* us.

"Hallo…? Are you listening to me, Maxie?"

My expression fell flat, but I nodded. I sopped up the rest of my stew with a biscuit and stuffed it in my mouth, then drained the rest of my drink. The stubborn little chin I'd once adored now left me wary, and I rubbed my hand against my neck. As she turned her wrist from side to side, I glanced at her bracelet.

"Hey, I'm sorry I haven't thanked you for the charm. Every time I went to call you about it, or stop by the office, well…" Her voice trickled to a whisper. "I wimped out, I guess."

"It's okay. I just wondered if you liked it, and if it helped ease the loss…a little anyway."

Ashley nodded, then turned her wrist over, displaying the ruby and gold Scottish Terrier charm I'd bought her over a week ago and had delivered to the house. She rubbed her finger over it gingerly. "Yes, I love it. I'll never forget what she meant to us."

I lowered my head, muttering a quiet, "Good."

Ashley slid her glass to the side of the table and grabbed hold of my hand. "This is a big deal, Maxie. Even though we're not married anymore, you're still the best man I know, and you deserve this kind of recognition. Let me help you."

I carefully retrieved my hand and pushed my plate aside. I lowered my brows, meeting her gaze. "Go on. Tell me what you've got planned."

As Ashley rattled off the details for the evening of dinner, drinks, and pitching, I questioned—for one deeply disturbing moment—whether I should tell Goldie about this. *What the hell?* I wanted to kick myself in my own ass. She deserved the truth. *Especially when it involves Ashley.* Several minutes passed then I dropped a few bills on the table, grabbed the pastry bag, and ushered my ex-wife from the diner.

Outside on the sidewalk, she turned to me and squeezed my arm. "So, I'll meet you tomorrow night at Ironside's Grill. Seven thirty sharp."

I glanced down at her hand, noting the familiar square-shaped nails polished seashell pink, then removed her fingers from my arm. "Okay."

Undeterred, she came in for a hug. "You're going to wow him, Maxie. I know it. I'll see you tomorrow."

Moments later, standing stock-still, I watched Ashley make her way across the parking lot and hop in her car. My thoughts blurred, the blood practically whooshing between my ears. *Me. My ex-wife. And one very lucrative deal at stake.* I shoved my hands in my pants pocket. *Of course, I'm going to tell Goldie about the pitch dinner.* I twisted the leather bead bracelet between my fingers. *So, why the hell haven't I told her about the MerryBelle charm?*

****

My walk back to the office took twice the usual time, but then my day had gone from routine to mind-boggling in the course of an hour. People with their noses glued to their cell phones buzzed by me on the sidewalk, occasionally brushing my elbow as I mentally kicked the can down the road. Tension settled in my jaw, and I wiggled my chin against the tightness. Ashley always had a purpose behind her actions, and maneuvering this meeting was no exception. Even though she framed it as a favor for CDD, I felt like she'd pitchforked me in the process.

I bolted into our building, forgoing the elevator and taking the stairs by two. Ashley liked calling the shots, but she didn't like being labeled as controlling. Over the years I'd become efficient at reading her carefully crafted hints.

I grumbled under my breath as I hit the third flight, recalling the time she was itching for a Mexican vacation and bought us a subscription for a crash course in conversational Spanish. She even splurged on special swimwear, surprising me with a pair of navy trunks to coordinate with her navy and white floral one-piece. *And why the hell not?* Nothing screamed sexy vacay with your husband like matching nautical swimsuits. *But what did I do?* I took the hint and booked us a villa for two weeks in Cozumel.

When I reached my floor, I made my way to Sofia's door. She greeted me with a grunt, hitting me with a glare from above her glasses. I dangled the paper bag in the air.

"And don't even tell me you've brought something from Thomason's because with the way I'm feeling right now…?" Not bothering to wipe the frown off her face, she gave me an enter motion with her hand.

I dropped into the chair beside her desk and slid the bag toward her elbow. "Got you a cherry turnover. I hope it's okay—I know you're cutting back on chocolate." I read the little V on her forehead. "George mentioned it the other day."

She pulled her lip into her mouth, fighting a smile, and swung her gaze to the bag. "Thank you. I need this after what I've been doing for the last hour."

I spied the crisscross pile of invoices she was thumbing through and propped my chin in my hand. "Did you get a paper cut or something?"

Sofia stopped, dangling a canary piece of paper from her fingertips like a worm on a hook. "Not. Funny. Boss."

My face heated at her jab. *I've been sideswiped enough for one day, thank you very much.* I rolled my shoulders, conceding this was Sofia, the one who'd resuscitated me when my marriage flatlined. *Still, I have my pride.*

I snatched the paper from her hand—an invoice from Andersen's Jewelers—and flicked it nonchalantly. "What? I put them on my personal account."

"Duh, I know how to pay for them. I just can't figure out why you'd buy them."

"Sorry, is knowing why a part of your job?" I asked, deadpanning.

Sofia exhaled deeply, crossing her arms on the desktop. "No. But it's something a friend would ask another friend—even her boss."

An essential oil diffuser hummed at the corner of her desk, and I breathed in deeply. She slid it closer to me. "It's a new blend called 'Raindrops on Ice.' "

I arched my brows. "Huh. Shouldn't that be 'Raindrops on Roses?' "

She chuckled from behind the palm of her hand. "Uh, that's a song, Max. This is aromatherapy."

I nodded once, then dropped the invoice on her desk. I began fiddling with some paper clips in a dish, linking them together. The silence between us took on a life of its own, interrupted only by the crinkling of the paper bag as she opened it.

I shrugged one shoulder. "The necklace is for Goldie."

"Very nice."

"And I bought the charm on impulse. That's it. End of story."

Sofia broke the turnover in two and offered me a half. We chewed in silence until she paused, reaching for some napkins from the bag. "And what exactly did you hope to gain from buying your ex-wife an expensive charm of a Scottish Terrier?"

At the judgelike tone of her question, I polished off the pastry, wiping my mouth on a napkin and folding my arms across my chest. "You haven't seen Ashley, okay? She's been a freaking wreck. Losing MerryBelle has been really…bad," I said, swallowing what felt like a fist of porcupine quills.

Sofia leaned in closer. "Look, I know it's been hard. I mean, you gave Merry to Ashley, and she stuck with you guys through the divorce." She finished her turnover then tossed the bag in the wastebasket. "I'm just concerned you've been to see Ashley, and now you've given her this gift…? We both know how easily you take on responsibility, but with her, are you sure you know what you're doing?"

As I thought about Ashley touching my hand at the diner and her well-timed intervention into my business affairs, the weight pressing down on my shoulders grew heavier.

"No. Not really," I said, my voice dropping an octave. I looked at my watch, thankful my weekly appointment was just an hour away. *But I know who will.*

****

"But that's stupid, right?" I felt my eyebrow lift in amusement, then Andy met my gaze for one brief moment and proceeded to fold his hands over his stomach.

Or not.

I shifted in the overstuffed chair, holding my counselor's little league baseball and studying the stitches. Andy kept the ball in a stand on the corner of his desk, and I'd spotted it right away at my first counseling session. My gaze swung to his gallery wall and the dozen old comic books displayed in frames. If his baseball hadn't won me over that day, his collection sure had. I mean, what two guys wouldn't connect over baseball and superheroes…and of course, my shit-show life.

I dragged my gaze in Andy's direction. Another thing I liked was the way he looked the part of the counselor without actually *looking* like one. In his early forties, he wore wire-rimmed glasses, department store khakis, and black cross-trainers. He rocked when it came to giving me think time, and he had few quirks…just the occasional finger tap on the temple of his glasses. I felt at ease coming to the building he shared with three of his colleagues, a 1920's rustic brownstone featuring a restoration of the original fireplace. Inside his office, he kept a simple desk in the corner, this pair of overstuffed chairs—no couch—near the large bay window, and his pickleball gear by the door.

I palmed the baseball and looked at him. "So I gave Ashley a charm to remember our dog. Doesn't mean anything."

And there he goes doing his finger tapping thing.

Then he surprised me, pulling off the glasses and laying them on the coffee table.

"There's no rule against giving your ex-wife a gift, especially during a time of grief. You made a conscious decision to do it. Why are you questioning your motives now? Or maybe the better question is *who's* causing you to doubt them."

I tossed the ball from my right hand to my left. *Smack.* From my left to my right. *Smack.* I cycled through a few more rounds then put the baseball on the table with a thud.

"If I were alone, the gift wouldn't matter. But I'm not. Alone."

Andy reached for a couple of waters, offering me one. I uncapped it, tilting my head back for a drink.

"So you're feeling guilty?"

"Yeah. A little."

"Yet you claimed it didn't mean anything."

I knew Andy was only doing his job, but his question felt like salt on a cut. I averted my gaze, glancing at his gallery of comic books. How I wished my problems could be solved with something as simple as a red cape or some ancient amulet.

I blew out my breath. "It's the secret, okay? Not the gift. It's my keeping a secret from Goldie." I lowered my voice. "I'm not sure she'll understand why I gave it to Ashley."

Andy regarded me for a few long seconds then shrugged. "And she never will. At least, not until you give her the chance to try."

Fuck a duck. Here comes the whole vulnerability thing again, jumping up to take a bite out of my ass. What I felt for Goldie was different, and our relationship was different. But there couldn't be real intimacy without trusting her.

"I need to tell her about the gift, don't I?" I watched Andy pick up the baseball, waiting while he rubbed his thumbs over the stitching. And I continued to wait because I really wanted his confirmation.

"Is that what you want to do?"

"Hell no. I don't want to hurt Goldie's feelings…and I don't want her to leave me."

"So you think keeping this secret is good for her and your relationship in the long run?"

Coming out of my counselor's mouth, my rationale sounded twisted, delusional even. I leaned forward, elbows on my thighs. "Is it so wrong I want to protect her and what we have? Keep her happy? I can take the hit and keep the stupid charm thing a secret. It's only going to cause trouble."

Andy wedged the baseball under his chin, his expression turning reflective. "Do you remember when you first told me about your rowing team in college and how you sat in the stroke seat?" I nodded, vaguely intrigued, somewhat baffled. "Of the eight rowers in the boat, tell me again who the coach puts in that position."

I sat up straighter. "The strongest competitor, a good communicator. The stroke sets the team's rhythm and stroke rate."

"Did running a good race fall on your shoulders?"

"It's a team sport, Andy. Every position counts."

"Indulge me."

Shit. Here we go.

"Like the pitcher, the quarterback, the point guard…the stroke is the leader, the one everyone knows will take the hard hits if it means protecting his teammates and the win." I cleared my throat. "So yeah, running a good race fell on my shoulders."

Andy arched his eyebrows. "That's not entirely different from the oldest brother who watches over, cleans up after, and forgives his younger siblings when they mess up."

"What you're saying is I'm a damn control freak, hung up on protecting the people I care about?" I shook my head. "All I was looking for was a thumbs-up—that I needed to tell Goldie the truth."

Andy lobbed the baseball at me, and I caught it with

one hand.

"No, Max. What I'm saying is you don't need my blessing. You're a leader, a provider, and a protector. You know the right choice is seldom an easy one. Bottom line, only one confirmation matters—the one that comes from inside *you*."

I fell back in my chair, and this time I was the one wedging the baseball underneath my chin. Ashley loved her charm bracelet, and when I saw the little terrier charm at the jewelry store that day, it spoke to me. But keeping the gift a secret from Goldie had made my gut hurt for a week. Goldie deserved better, and I wanted to be better…for her.

I tossed the baseball back to Andy, and he caught it with both hands. "I'm going to tell Goldie about the gift and apologize for not telling her sooner. I don't want secrets between us, and I have to believe she'll forgive me somehow."

Andy smiled, and for a brief moment his grin reminded me of how my dad looked when he was my coach and I hit a homerun. Dad smiled the same way when my rowing team took first place, or I snagged another account for the company.

As I closed the door to Andy's office and walked outside, my step was lighter than it'd been a few hours ago. Sessions like today, where the gloves came off and a little blood got spilled, were what kept me coming back every week.

And now I know what I have to do.

Chapter Nineteen

Wednesday, June 23rd 11:15 p.m.
Goldie

Sex before Max was like staring at a landscape painted in shades of taupe and gray. I snuggled against him, loving the feel of skin to skin. But sex *with* Max was like being engulfed in a kaleidoscope of fuchsia, violet, and cerulean blue. *A masterpiece.*

Through many weeks of incredible lovemaking, I'd discovered an obstacle course in the rips and hard planes of his body. With my head resting on his abdomen, I slid my hand over his muscular thigh on a questing caress to the knotty scar on his right knee. I turned my head to press a kiss on his navel, then gazed down at his size-twelve feet. I smiled at the rather long second toes peeking out from beneath the sheet, the same toes I loved in the flip-flops he wore when we walked through the garden. A soft sigh slipped from my lips with the revelation Max wasn't a completely flawless male. *But he is completely male.*

My head moved with the ragged rise and fall of his chest. I waited, and the next breath came in a similar rush. I turned, folding my arms across the ropes of his abdominal muscles, chin on my hands. "I hear you thinking."

Max trailed his thumb across my cheek. "Making love to you is like nothing I've ever known. I'm still reeling from it."

My face warmed with the memory, a blur of hips and pelvis thrusting into me. I loved how whenever we were joined, his gaze never left mine. My brow suddenly creased. *But not tonight...*

Tonight, mantled over me with his eyes closed, he'd buried his face in my neck when he groaned his release.

I swallowed hard. "You set off skyrockets inside me, too. Every time."

"I hope so."

"You know so, because you're always watching me." I took his hand in mine. "Until tonight anyway." As his fingers flinched, my throat went all scratchy. "I-I didn't realize it in the moment. Only now...with your heavy breathing and all..."

He dropped my hand, grabbing a pillow and shoving it between his shoulders and the headboard. I fell back on one elbow, pulling the sheet over my breasts. His mouth fell into a flat line, and he brushed a lock of hair behind my shoulders, offering a simple, "It's nothing."

Only when something's really *something does your boyfriend—lying naked with you in bed—say 'it's nothing.'* I sat up, hiding my trembling hands in the sheet. The degree of my alarm surprised even me. "No, I think it's something."

A crease furrowed his brow.

"And don't look at me like that, like you're trying to spare my feelings. If you're leav—"

"You're right," Max said, pushing out an audible breath. "I need to tell you something."

Oh, God...

Every inky black cloud I'd ever walked under paled against this one. I blinked against the tears stinging my eyes, digging my fingernails into my palms with such might I was sure they'd leave marks. I gazed at his mouth, his lips pursed as if contemplating something weighty, but it was hard to tell, as his expression was innately intense.

Max raked his hand through his hair then opened his arm in invitation. "Come here, Goldie. Please?"

As always, his persuasive green eyes worked their magic, and I went to him. I slipped my hand in the gap between his reclined shoulders and the pillow. He stroked the soft skin at the bend of my elbow with his thumb and pressed a kiss to the top of my head. I knew he wouldn't tell me he loved me on the way out the door. *Because you've never used the word with me.*

My gaze narrowed at the scant bit of moonlight piercing through the blinds, and inwardly I shuddered. Max's 'nothing' would likely cut my feet out from under me and drop me on my ass.

****

Max

My blunt words cut in a way I hadn't intended. Goldie's eyes creased at the corners, long lashes shadowing her darkening irises. *Fuck.*

I'd rationalized waiting to tell her about the charm, wanting to make love to her once more before she likely hightailed it out of my life, cursing my dishonesty. I sliced my fingers through my hair, disgusted with myself. I'd behaved no better than your average drunk, needing his fix and blindly reaching for it. And Goldie had nailed me on it.

Time to come clean and take my lumps.

I couldn't help wanting to touch her. It was impossible not to. When she fell into my open arms, I said a silent prayer of thanks. I pressed my lips to the top of her head and began lifting the burden from my heart.

I thought her breathing would race when I told her about Ashley cornering me at lunch, but it didn't.

I expected her to stiffen in my arms when I revealed her business dinner plans for Thursday night, but she didn't.

I imagined the words 'emotional misfit' rolling off her tongue when I confessed buying the Scottish Terrier charm, but they didn't.

I watched the ceiling fan circling above us, counting the seconds until Goldie said something...anything. I continued breathing, waiting, this strange new vulnerability feeling like a foreign language to me. I raised my fist to my forehead, reasoning I could no more alter my nature than reorder the days of the week. But to keep Goldie in my life, I'd sure as hell give it my best shot.

Goldie squeezed my shoulder with her fingers. "I can still hear you thinking."

"About you? Yes. Yes, I am. And I'm waiting— patiently for as long as you need—to tell me how bad I've screwed up."

She worked a pillow to her liking, then settled against it, resting her head in her hand. "I-I thought you were breaking up with me."

My gaze tracked across her face, so unbelievably honest and exposed, and I covered her free hand with mine.

"Yeah," she murmured. "When we were making love, I never saw your eyes. Then, it hit me because I love how you're always watching us. All I could think was you were tired of me."

"God, no. Never."

"I know, it's my baggage—I'll deal with it." She lowered her gaze, lashes fanned against her cheeks.

I lifted her chin with my finger. "No, we'll talk about it. Together. You're my beautiful, bossy, brainy girl. You're more than enough for me, more than I deserve. I'm the one who let you down." I rolled onto my side, facing her. "Please, yell at me. Do anything...except leave."

Goldie flopped back on the mattress. "I promised to be honest with you, but you have to promise me the same." Her fingers clutched the sheet, and she cut her gaze at me. "Do I wish you'd told me about the gift from the start? Yeah, I do. I'm not cold-hearted, Max. I would've understood how hard Ashley was taking Merry's death and the meaning behind the gift." She paused for a breath, shaking her head. "But I don't know—now she's planning this fancy schmancy dinner—pushing into your business and your life?"

I smiled on the inside, unable to recall anyone under the age of fifty ever using the phrase 'fancy schmancy,' but the expression suited her. I slid closer to her. "You're right. I was looking for something else at Andersen's, and I spotted the charm by chance. I thought it might bring Ashley some peace. But that doesn't change the fact I should've told you straight away. I promise that won't happen again." I kissed her knuckles, then met her gaze. "And as far as the dinner goes, I told her I'd be there...only I didn't tell her I'd come alone. You could join me."

Goldie turned to me, worrying her lip between her teeth. "No. No, this is too important to risk playing games. You need to be there representing CDD with a clear head. I'm good with it. Just don't keep me in the dark anymore…about anything, okay?"

"I promise."

"I trust you, and I'm not leaving."

"Thank God." I held her face in my hands, my thumbs stroking her cheeks. "It feels so much better to share things with you. I've got a long way to go with opening up, I know. But I'll get there—I'm sure of it— because no one's ever meant so much to me. Please tell me you know that."

She nodded, a hint of a smile teasing at her lips, and tucked her hands between her cheek and the pillow.

"Now I hear *you* thinking."

"Hm, mind-read much, Mr. Corda?"

"Only you, Peach." I pulled her against me. "Let me guess. I bet you were wondering why I was at Andersen's Jewelers." Her eyes sparkled, making me feel like the luckiest man alive. "I was saving this for a special occasion." I swiveled around, pulling a black velvet necklace box out of my nightstand. "Like tonight."

She let out a tiny gasp, her eyes wide with wonder. I helped her sit up, and the bed sheet pooled around her waist. "But I'm naked."

"I know. You're perfect," I murmured. "May I?"

Looking like Venus herself, Goldie nodded. As I dragged my gaze from the exquisite view of her body to the box in my hand, my chest grew tight. I'd wanted to make love to her since the day we met, but over the past month, I'd learned I wanted to please her, too. I liked how she sighed deeply when I massaged her feet with lotion after a bubble bath and how in the mornings, her nose twitched with the scent of the ginger green tea I had steeping in a cup on her nightstand.

And there's the real kicker. It was her nightstand, beside our bed, inside what I was quickly discovering was our home. I couldn't deny it. After baring my conscience to her tonight, I realized she was well and truly meant for me.

Goldie turned so I could fasten the necklace at her nape, and as she came around again, I hoped the pearl and diamond pendant would lay right at the hollow of her throat. *It does...perfectly.*

"Oh my God, Max. I've never seen anything more beautiful..."

"I have. And I'm looking right at her." I pulled her to me, pouring my feelings into the kisses I pressed along the curve of her neck. Her tiny sighs released the tightness in my chest, replacing it with an urgency to push every doubt from her mind. I moved over her, sheltering her with my body, and when our gazes locked, I began making love to her.

Chapter Twenty

Thursday, June 24th 1:45 p.m.
Goldie

I leaned against the bathroom counter and dragged a cold washcloth across my face. Though my headache had lessened to a dull throbbing, my stomach felt like it'd been flattened by an eighteen-wheeler. When I straightened, my reflection in the mirror confirmed I was indeed a casualty from a head-on collision.

I was swishing mouthwash in my mouth when the doorbell rang. I peeked at the unopened texts on my phone, dawning lighting my face when I read the one from Sofia.

—*I'm taking a late lunch. I've got saltines and ginger ale.*—

I padded across the floor, opening the door with an exhausted hello.

"Boy, looks like I got here just in time. You look terrible." Sofia dragged out the last word, brushing past me with her arms full. "Not going to lie, I'm surprised to find you here. I went by the condo first."

I pressed my palm over my forehead. "Ugh, can you blame me? I'd rather puke in my old toilet and pass out on my linoleum floors than make a mess at Max's place."

She nodded. "Max was beside himself when I told him you got sick at work. He practically sprinted out the door, but I asked him to trust me and not clear out the rest of his day. I told him I'd take care of you…which is what friends are for, right?" she added with a wink.

I followed her to my bedroom and slid under the covers. I propped my pillows against the headboard and leaned back, rehashing the last few hours since I'd fled the office with a trash bag in my hand.

She slipped a straw inside a can of ginger ale and handed me a cracker. "Are you sure you're all right? A ghost has more color than you."

I sipped the soda, waving the cracker in the air. "Yeah, well, I guess we'll know if I keep this down, right?"

"True that." Sofia smiled, then pulled the chair at my dressing table to the bed. "Any idea what made you sick?"

"Physically, no. We had a grilled shrimp salad for supper last night. I had avocado with toast for breakfast and some edamame for a snack."

She wrinkled her nose. "Another reason why I skip all the nature food and take vitamin supplements."

I chuckled despite the ache in my tummy then nibbled on the cracker. "Oh, wow…these are insanely good." As Sofia passed me the whole sleeve of saltines, I felt a frown tugging at my lips. I tucked a strand of hair behind my ear. "But I know who made me emotionally sick."

She leaned closer, assessing me from above her glasses. "And by that do you mean Dr. Ashley Windrow-Corda?"

"Yeah…so do you suppose she's ever going to change her name?" I hated the possessive note clinging to my question. After all, she'd been his wife for nine years, and she'd earned her doctorate with the name. *But divorce changes things, right?*

"Maybe. But the Corda name is big in Charlotte. She's probably not ready to let go of it."

I wiped some crumbs off my chin with the back of my hand. "I guess you know the deal about the terrier charm."

"Yeah." She reached over to touch my arm. "It was a bone-headed thing to do, but Max said he only wanted to console her. I believe him."

I sipped my ginger ale. "I do, too. He's such a protector and nurturer. You should've seen the way he took care of Jack's children when we were on the Shembery trip. His heart's so big. I think it's what I love most about him."

Sofia settled back in her chair, pushing her sleeves over her elbows and crossing her arms over her chest. "You're in deep, Goldie Girl."

I instantly stopped chewing and nodded my head. As corny as it sounded, being in a relationship with Max had been like pulling a cork from a bottle of fine wine. Our connection was rich and aromatic, our relationship—and God, the sex—was delicious. *He never leaves me wanting.* I sighed, chasing the crackers with more ginger ale, quite certain I'd never be happy with wine from a box ever again.

"You look like you're in pain—and I don't mean from all the hurling you've been doing."

"Try contemplative."

"Well, if you happen to be *contemplating* this pitch dinner tonight, I can promise you the university is a fish Max and Mr. Corda have wanted for a long time. Our designs are in municipalities and businesses all over the East Coast, but a project of this scale would be a first."

I placed the crackers on my nightstand and took another sip of my drink. "It's a no-brainer. If Ashley has the in-roads to help make this thing happen, then Max has to be there. With her."

"You okay with that?"

"If I am, then I come off looking like a woman who's confident—who's smart and trusts her boyfriend."

"And if you aren't?"

I groaned. "Then everyone will think I'm clingy and insecure."

"Everyone at work knows you're a classy, brilliant engineer. They also know you're gaga for the guy," she said, waving a finger at the protest forming on my lips. "But hold on. No one has ever seen Max so damn happy either. I think the tightrope he walked in his marriage made him forget his real worth. He's stopped with the late nights working. He steps off the elevator with a little swagger, you know?"

I bit my lower lip, hanging on the affirmation in her words.

"He's strolling around the office with his coffee, talking with people about things other than schematics and statistics."

"I had no idea."

She reached for a saltine, pointing it at me. "That's why I'm telling you this. You play in your corner of the sandbox, and you're never around Max except at team meetings. Some of us actually work closely with him and," she said, biting into the cracker, "he's a different person these days. Still doesn't mean he's perfect. Or that he might still need reminding to check his old habits with his ex-wife at the door."

"I don't want to become a nag."

She leaned closer, wiping a crumb from her chin. "You're a farm girl…so let me put it this way. Imagine Max as a gardener, and you're the pretty Goldenrod wildflower he loves. But Ashley—she's a prickly clump of weeds, always popping up and choking everything in sight." I raised both eyebrows, and she shushed me. "You can trust him though. Max the Gardener knows this weed *very* well and will do what needs to be done to keep it under control, because he'd do anything to take care of his Goldenrod."

My lips formed a smile. "I'm impressed. You slap with the metaphors."

"Why, thank you," she said. "My granny was always telling us stories to make sense of whatever crappy thing happened in our lives. Guess she rubbed off on me."

"Well, I've decided to trust Max."

She nodded once.

I took a long breath. "And I'm going to relax and support him with this dinner thing."

"And if I know Max, he'll come by here on his way to the restaurant."

I sat up straighter, wrinkling my nose when I sniffed my hair. "You know, I think the saltines are going to stay down. I'd like to get cleaned up, so would you mind hanging out until I get out of the shower?"

"Go on, I got this," she said, shooing me away. "I'd hate myself if I left and then heard you blacked out in the bathtub or something."

We shared a laugh then I shuffled to the bathroom.

****

After the shower and with my stomach settling, I slipped into fresh pajamas and opened the sliding door from the den to the back porch. I reclined on the sofa with more soda and crackers, enjoying the way the breeze caught the loose ends of hair from my messy bun. The sun hung low in the sky when my phone buzzed. *Max!* I picked it up. *Ace...?* I swiped it open.

"H-Hey, Ace," I said shakily.

"Hey...you all right?"

I pinched the bridge of my nose to hide a smile. Something in his question reminded me of the beehives on our farm and my dad's explanation that bees were so hypersensitive they could detect atmospheric electromagnetic waves. Even though Ace didn't have a bee's sense to warn of oncoming thunderstorms, he possessed more intuition than anyone else in our family. And God love him, he used it regularly on me.

"Good Lord, Ace. That's not much of a greeting."

"I can't help it. You sound like shit."

I sighed. "Well that's because I've been barfing up the contents of my stomach for most of the day." I detected his wince over the phone. "Yeah, it was gross."

"Better now though?"

"Yeah. Much." I pushed out a breath. "So...what's up with you?"

While I munched on crackers, I listened to Ace. He talked fast, ticking through the details of an idea he'd told me about last Christmas. The job involved a restoration of the farm's irrigation system, modernizing the structure and flow. While it was a substantial undertaking, he'd been planning and saving for it since Dad passed.

"I've got the financing terms how I want them. Now all I need is to get you on board."

"Me? Or CDD?"

"Both. But hey, I know you haven't been with the

firm very long. Just tell me who to contact so I can hire you on as our consultant for a few weeks."

I rambled through the backlog of accounts in my head. My stomach fluttered, and not from queasiness. I was excited to take on the project, and safeguarding the renovation to Three Creeks was a bonus.

"So…can you help your big brother?"

"Let me check on things with Ethan. It's possible," I said, stretching out the word, "they could send me there after the July Fourth holiday."

"Hell, yes. That's perfect for the timing with the bank."

"Now don't hold me to anything. Let me talk to Ethan first."

"Have I told you lately how proud I am of you?"

I shifted on the sofa, tucking my feet underneath me. "Yeah, but I never get tired of hearing it. It's been a good move for me, Ace. So many things are happening."

"You sounded rough earlier. They're not working you too hard, are they? Outside of a few texts, I haven't heard from you since you got back from Shembery."

"No, they're not. I've just been busy."

"You been making more friends, like that one Sofia?"

I remained silent, perhaps for a bit too long.

"Goldie?"

I squeezed my eyes shut.

"Goldie…?" The timber of his voice tugged on my heart.

"I-I've kinda met someone."

"I knew it! Mom acted all weird last week when I mentioned you coming here to oversee the project. She said you were too busy, but I didn't buy it. Why didn't you tell me?"

"Honestly…? I don't even know. I've only told Mom and Prim, and Sofia, of course." I could practically hear his thoughts ticking over the phone, and it killed me.

"I get you wanting to talk with them first, but this is me, Golds. I love you more than anything. You know you've got your fist around my heart."

I smiled, remembering the first time Ace ever said that to me. I was in middle school, and he'd come home from college for summer. When he overheard Kyle—the douchebag son of our mayor—teasing me after church one Sunday, he threatened to punch his lights out if he ever spoke to me like that again. The terror etched on Kyle's face was the best, and the fact a dozen of our friends saw it…? *Perfection.* And from then on, Ace liked to say since I had a fist around his heart, the least he could do was use his to protect me. *You still make me feel like the most special girl in the world.*

"I love you, too, and I want to tell you about him. His name is Max. And Ace, he's absolutely *amazing*…"

Chapter Twenty-One

Thursday, June 24th 3:50 p.m.
Max

I cupped Goldie's cheeks with my palms, rubbing my thumbs on her skin. "How are you doing, Peach?" I kissed her brow, thankful she wasn't fevered. "Sofia's right. You're pale."

"Could be because I just washed the makeup off my face," she offered with a weak smile. "I'm doing better. Honest. I've eaten an entire pack of saltines and polished off two ginger ales. Hopefully, the worst has passed."

"I'm so glad. I wanted to come the minute I heard, but Sofia convinced me not to."

"Glad you listened to her. The last thing I wanted was to be sick in front of anyone, except maybe my mom."

I chuckled. "Moms really are the best at that sort of thing, aren't they? But hey, you'd better get used to me being around. I like taking care of you."

As I rubbed my hands over her arms, she stepped closer, pressing her cheek against my chest. I embraced her, my breathing falling into sync with hers, and for a few moments Ashley's maneuvering for this big kahuna university deal seemed vague and nondescript. Goldie needed me. I bent to kiss the top of her head. *You're quickly becoming home to me.* She smelled like clean soap and mint, and I wished I could keep her in the circle of my arms forever.

I released a slow breath with her name. "Goldie?" I felt her head tip upward beneath my chin. "I wish I didn't have to go tonight. I can't explain it, but I don't like Ashley's influence in this."

She sighed. "I know and thank you for saying that. But this could be big, and I support you one hundred ten percent. You're going to nail it, Max."

I leaned back and let my gaze travel over her body, from her rumpled shorty pajamas and slipper socks to her hair clouded around her shoulders. Instinctively, I brushed a few loose strands away from her face, the effects of the stomach bug visible in her hollow cheeks.

I thought about what Sofia told me before I left the office this afternoon. *I dropped a dress size last time I had the stomach flu.* When I'd mentioned bringing Goldie some of Thomason's chicken noodle soup after the dinner meeting, she suggested I make some myself. *Nothing complicated. Fix her the kind from a can, mixed with water…and a lot of TLC.*

Goldie coughed, and the sound fired my protective nature. "May I come by after the meeting? I could fix you some chicken noodle soup or maybe some oatmeal? Whatever you want." My chest expanded on a breath, and I spoke straight from my heart. "Please, let me take care of you."

Our gazes locked for a lingering moment, then she said, "Okay. I've got some cans of soup in the cabinet. I'd really like that."

I hugged her close. *My girl needs me.*

****

Once seated at Ironside's, I sipped on a gin and tonic while waiting for my party to arrive. The place was an icon in Charlotte, a saloon and grill founded post-prohibition. History had it Jock Ironside, after a law enforcement career spent chasing bootleggers across the county, opened the place with his son, a veteran of World War II, at Christmastime 1945.

Both locals and visitors flocked to the prime midtown destination. *And who could blame them?* The restaurant featured a marble staircase with an iron-spindled rail leading to a small upstairs dining room. On the main level, three carved glass panels separated a mahogany bar from the large dining room.

Over the years, they'd curated the collection of antique beer steins and cuckoo clocks on display in the bar, and it was rumored the array of animal heads on the walls were nailed by the old man himself. In their seventy-fifth anniversary celebration a few years back, fourth generation owner Joanna Ironside-Nichols commissioned a local artisan to etch images of her great-grandfather, grandfather, and father in the three glass panels. Seated in a booth with black velvet upholstery, gazing at the impressive glass etchings across the room and antique chandeliers hanging from the high ceilings, I hoped the Corda family legacy in Charlotte would one day enjoy Ironside's caliber of longevity.

I soon spotted Ashley entering the dining room alongside Vice-Chancellor Pennington. I watched her approach, hair swinging in time with her step, blunt ends brushing her cheek until—*yep, there she goes*—she curled her finger around the lock.

When I stood to shake hands with Greer, Ashley slipped past, sliding into my side of the booth. She settled in on my right, exchanging smiles between me and the man who'd been my sixth grade Sunday school teacher with the grace of a swan floating across a lake. As she ordered her usual—filet mignon with garlic-sauteed spinach—her hand dropped to my knee. The movement sent a prickly sensation through my leg, and my gaze flickered to hers. As understanding dawned, the corners of her eyes softened, and she withdrew her hand.

With the three of us being friends, we ordered appetizers and drinks, swapping a few stories about our families. Soon after, Greer began elaborating on the key physical drivers in the university's comprehensive infrastructure plan. Based on needs assessment data and feedback from their stakeholders, the board of trustees was committed to optimizing both land and natural resources to create a compelling and sustainable campus experience. They were leveraging main campus systems—from stormwater to open space utilization for pedestrian traffic—to bring vital change to the university community.

By the time the server brought our entrees, I had a handle on the plan, identifying a recurring theme in Greer's remarks. The university envisioned a legacy—a sort of *cohesive* geography—that would continually shape how people came to interact with the campus well into the next century. I nodded my agreement. *This vision of sustainability is tailored for CDD.*

As the ever-strategic swan, Ashley reminded Greer over dessert a renovation of this scale would place the university in a favorable position for various environmental tax incentives. I smiled inwardly, unruffled by her poise and ability to tick off a short list of such programs the way others might recite the alphabet.

Greer took a bite of carrot cake, waving his fork

between us. "What gets me is how well you two still play off each other. Makes me wonder what the hell drove you apart."

Ashley held her wineglass in her hand, lips pursed in contemplation. "God, I don't even know if *we* know the answer. Maybe we were too much alike. Seems there wasn't much room for anything besides our dueling ambitions, wouldn't you say, Max?"

I wiped my cloth napkin over the frown tugging at my lips. Once upon a time, Ashley was my closest friend, and she won my heart the day she made me that bracelet. What I realized now was our marriage died incrementally, cozy interludes the collateral damage with two people singularly focused on carving out 'the dream.' About the time I turned thirty and figured out she no longer wanted to be saddled with an emotional misfit, I realized I wasn't afraid of growing old and dying one day. I was already dying because I should've been out there, alive and kicking.

I dropped my napkin on the table, pushed out a quiet breath, and nodded. "Yeah, I'd say that about sums it up."

Ashley turned to Greer with a gleam in her eye. "You remember the gala Max and CDD underwrote for the Foundation a few years back? Max and I worked lockstep on it, and we scored big on new endowments for the college of business."

"Indeed. You're a regular dynamic duo," Greer said with a nod, turning to me. "Well, you're wise to remain friends after the divorce. Your paths are bound to cross from time to time, and you don't want things to be awkward." He placed his fork on his plate and pushed it aside. "And remember, Max, the deadline for the proposal is July fifteenth."

"Good thing this has been on his radar for some time. And after tonight's conversation," Ashley said, reaching over to squeeze my forearm, "I'm confident his bid will outshine all the others."

Despite the tightening in my stomach with Ashley's touch, my competitive juices kicked in, and I folded my hands into a single fist on the tabletop. "You already know CDD's reputation for excellence, and if we come in with the winning bid, you can trust every schematic, every design decision will meet the Trustees' expectations. Now, as to the dynamic duo part…?" I said, my gaze swinging to my ex-wife, "I think Ashley will agree we never compromise in business."

Soon the three of us made our way to the front lobby and said our goodbyes. Ashley stood beside me, both of our gazes tracking Greer as he left the restaurant. She turned, throwing her arms around my neck. I stumbled backward, embracing her to stabilize us. *What the hell?*

"I haven't had that much fun in forever," Ashley said, dragging out the last word.

I drew my brows down, my gaze resting on her forearms pressed against my chest. She slid her fingers around to the knot in my tie, tugging gently. I waited, and when she met my gaze, I watched her read the question in my eyes.

"What? I'm excited, and you should be, too. We've waited years for the university to get moving on the next phase of their master plan."

"I know how much you love the university and your job, but you're not usually so…" I paused, tossing around a few adjectives before landing on, "exuberant."

Her arms fell to her sides, and she straightened. "I

care about your company. I always have."

"Except when CDD interfered with your plans."

"Yeah, well, it interfered with your promise to be with me at my tenure celebration, didn't it? And I didn't give you hell about that."

"Not much, but that was only because Merry had just—"

"Died? Yes, yes, she had." She shifted, resting her hand on her hip. "Without you. Because you put work before us again…or maybe you bowed out because of your new girlfriend."

I didn't have the patience for her junk pitches tonight, so I made sure my next hit would fly clear out of the ballpark.

"You know I'll always care about you. But we're *divorced*, which means our relationships are strictly off-limits." I lowered my voice a degree. "You also know I intended to keep my promise. But I won't stand here and apologize for my loyalty to the company. I had to deliver to the client what neither Ethan, Dad, nor James could. That's all. End. Of. Story."

Ashley folded her arms over her chest. "My God, Maxie. That was quite a mouthful." The smirk in her voice was unmistakable. "Why can't you just thank me for tonight and give me a hug?"

"Jesus," I groaned, scratching my head, a dozen emotions boomeranging through my brain. Had she always whiplashed me like this? Sadly, I thought the answer was yes. "Okay. Thank you, Ashley."

She lifted her chin. "Not, 'Thank you, *Ash*?' "

"No," I said, perhaps more coarsely than I would've liked. It wasn't like her to tease, much less flirt. Our rules of engagement had been honed over the years, and I saw no point in a detour. "I appreciate what you did to make tonight happen, *Ashley*. Even if we don't land the account, thank you for supporting my company."

She tilted her head, toying with her diamond stud earring. "Let's go to the bar for a drink—for old time's sake."

"No." This time my tone was purposely coarse.

"Oh," she said, as if unveiling a mystery. "Got the girlfriend waiting back at your place, huh?"

"Is that what this is really about?" I barked over a laugh.

"I stick my neck out for you, and this is how you treat me? Like some itch you don't feel like scratching?"

"We just gave a damn good impression of an amicably divorced couple. Why are you whiplashing me like this?" As her mouth dropped, I raised a cautionary hand. "And don't give me some crap about our similarities and *dueling ambitions*."

I knew I hit a nerve, and I didn't care. Ashley placed her palms on her hips, gaze flickering to my pants pocket. "Tell me…do you still keep it with you?"

My neck warmed, and I shook my head. "Stop deflecting my question."

She lifted her hand to brush away the lock of hair that'd fallen across my brow. "I can't help but wonder if I slipped my hand inside your pocket—"

"Stop it, Ash." I stilled her hand with mine.

"Ah ha," she said, practically purring. "You called me *Ash*."

I silently cursed my careless slip, pushing her hand away. "I'm leaving."

"Not before you turn out your pockets."

I stood motionless for several seconds, gawking at

her like she was some wall of screws in a hardware superstore. I was unhinged, and with a multitude of choices, I couldn't pinpoint what I needed to fix this mess. I combed her expression for any sign of understanding, and finding none, groaned under my breath. *I couldn't find the right damn screw if my life depended on it.*

She took a step toward me, meeting my gaze as though she'd felt me studying her. "Forget it. I have my answer."

"For fuck's sake, it's just a scrap of leather with some beads."

"No, Max. It's not."

A couple brushed by us, and I instinctively pulled Ashley over to the side. From the bar, the sounds of laughter and glasses clinking filled the air, but the word 'Max' hovered between us.

Not, Maxie.

My name tumbled through my head, rumbling like chains raising a medieval drawbridge against an oncoming enemy.

"It's a crutch," she said with a quiet sigh. "I should know. You've been mine for months. I was leaning on you for the tenure banquet. And then after losing Merry, crying on your shoulder again and again. And even tonight, wanting to have a drink with you–keeping you here with me."

I rubbed my hands over my eyes and pushed out a breath. In one respect, I needed her acknowledgement of the pressure she'd placed on me post-divorce. But in another, this wasn't about her. She'd thrown down the gauntlet, by God.

Yes, the bracelet habit needed breaking. *But it's not*

a damn crutch.

"Let me get this straight. First, you label me an *emotional misfit*. And now," I said, the acid in my voice intensifying, "you accuse me of being some—some *lovesick lunatic* because I've held on to a memento?"

"If it wasn't a crutch, you wouldn't be reacting this way."

I rolled my eyes at her.

"You'll never be free until you get rid of the bracelet." Ashley straightened, grabbing both my hands in hers. "I'm sorry—really, I am. I hate how awful I was to you when we were married, but what I want now is for you to be happy. I hoped this dinner, this inroad with the university, might make amends. I mean it."

"I'm not having this conversation with you. It's not a crutch. I don't *need* a crutch." I raised my index finger and added for clarity, "But what I do need is an ex-wife who'll stay in her lane and stop sticking it to me every chance she gets."

"Maxie, please—"

"Don't. Don't call me that." Worry creased her forehead, and I leaned in closer. "I'm Max."

Before she could mount another offensive, I turned for the door. Outside, I sucked in gulps of night air, pacing the length of the restaurant while the valet went for my car.

Police sirens blaring off in the distance stopped me dead in my tracks. I stared into the darkness, the few streetlamps around Ironside's creating more shadows than illumination. *Christ…did Ashley drive or get a lift here?* I took a deep breath.

Boyfriend Max would've called a cab to drive her home. *Like I did when I was away at a rowing tournament, and she phoned me after a late night at the library.*

Fiancé Max would've offered her a ride. *Like when I figured she wouldn't feel like walking from her job at the campus bistro back to her apartment after the evening shift.*

Husband Max would've insisted on driving her home and tucking her underneath a blanket on the couch. *Damn it.*

I trudged back into the restaurant, making my way through the crowded entryway, but as I crossed into the main bar, my stride slowed. From across the room, I spotted Ashley seated elbow to elbow with a man waving two fingers between them and the bartender. I recognized the guy from one of Ashley's departmental Christmas parties a few years back. He was a hard one to forget, sporting the same beard and bowtie, only tonight he'd left the red vest covered with reindeer faces at home. My gaze lingered on them for a few long beats before they raised their glasses in some shared toast, and his arm dropped over the back of her barstool.

I cocked my head, relieved the idea of Ashley dating didn't trip any alarms in me. There was no skip in the hum of my heart and body, both still sending their steady signals to my brain.

But with Goldie? *Oh, hell no.*

The mere suggestion of another man stealing her attention crushed into my chest. The depth of my reaction stirred something inside me. While jealousy had never clouded my thoughts about Ashley, I felt a rainstorm of it with Goldie. From behind the bar, a trio of Ironside's cuckoo clocks broke into a hooting chorus, and I shook my head.

What was ex-husband, emotional misfit, lovesick lunatic Max going to do for Ashley? I pivoted and made my way to the door. "Not a damn thing."

As I stepped outside, the valet arrived with my car, and I stuffed a few bills in his hand. Once inside, I punched the dashboard display for our playlist then typed a text.

—*On my way, Peach.*—

I waited for her reply, but seeing no little dots, I set my phone on the console and cranked the engine. I hit the accelerator and merged into traffic, heading toward her place.

I swore under my breath, hating the truth in Ashley's words. I couldn't be the man Goldie deserved as long as I held on to that sentimental scrap of leather. Andy's words from yesterday rambled through my mind, too. *Only one confirmation matters, Max.* I swallowed hard, realizing I had one last confession inside me. Then it'd be over...no more secrets.

As I turned into her apartment complex, I parked in the open spot beside her car. I'd never suffered a broken heart, but I knew without question, Goldie had the power to snap mine in half.

Chapter Twenty-Two

Friday, June 25th 7:05 a.m.
Goldie

I awoke to sunshine filtering through the sheers at my window, the most incredible memories of last night washing through me. The first one was of Max making me the best can of chicken noodle soup I'd ever tasted. The next? Max undressing me, giving me a hot bath, toweling me off, and then spooning behind me all night long. The snuggling almost made puking up my stomach lining worth it.

I heard the hallway floors creaking under footsteps, and moments later, Max appeared at my bedroom door with a breakfast tray. I scooted back toward the headboard then he placed it over my lap, the scent of ginger green tea teasing my nose. I squeezed in fresh lemon while he drizzled honey on the bowl of warm steel-cut oats.

I grinned at him. "You get an A plus for presentation."

"You like the heart-shaped line of honey, huh?"

"I do."

Max gazed into my eyes. "You feeling better?"

"Much."

He pressed a kiss on my forehead. "And for the record, I hate you being sick."

"I like you taking care of me."

"I hope so." His words sounded rusty to my ears, and I pulled back. He lifted his hand, brushing my hair behind my shoulders. I gazed at him, waiting to see where he was going with this, but he simply said, "You should eat your breakfast, Peach."

Max slid in beside me, reclining on a pillow and scrolling through his texts. Fueled by hunger and curiosity, I devoured my oatmeal, dropping my spoon in the bowl after my last bite. The clink snagged his attention, and he removed the tray, placing it on the floor. We turned to face each other, and he tucked the blanket around my waist.

"Hold me?" I asked, hating the neediness in my voice.

He pulled me into his arms, shifting a little left and right as though gauging how well we fit together. His thumb trailed idly over my shoulder, and I worked to steady my breathing. "So, last night you told me how well the business stuff went…but what about the rest?"

Max folded one arm behind his neck. "Not exactly what I expected." When I tilted my head up, I wasn't prepared for the faraway look in his eyes. A painful smile stretched across his mouth. "I knew Ashley would come off smooth and confident—the perfect liaison between me and Pennington." His gaze swept over my expression, then he added, "But she threw me a curveball."

His fingers slowed against my shoulder. I felt goose bumps prickling my skin, and I pushed away.

Only he followed me. "Are you okay?"

Hardly. I crossed my arms over my middle.

Just realizing my life is a pathetic game of Tag-You're It.

And there's no chance in hell I'll ever catch you, Max.

Because your ex-wife will see to it you're always just out of my reach.

I hunted for my voice. "That's awkward. Do I even want to know what you're talking about?"

Max shifted his weight, slid his hand into his pocket, and threw a crumpled brown leather band on the bed. It couldn't have been more stranger looking than if it'd been a crinkly insect with a pointy stinger or spotted wings. I rubbed the strap between my fingers, squinting to read the letters on the beads, and hoped it didn't bite.

Looking up, I waited until I caught his gaze. "Yeah, I think you'd better explain."

For the next few minutes, I watched Max pace across my bedroom while he spoke about distant memories, and even though I was just a few feet away, I'd never felt more isolated. I listened to every word, trying to tamp down thoughts about what wasn't enough in our relationship and to focus on what we had. At some point I simply stopped hearing his pleas, my heart shifting like tectonic plates on a fault line inside my chest. I was uncertain, unstable, and totally unprepared for the fallout.

When Max sat beside me, covering my hand with his, I snatched it away. My gaze grew hot. "This is what you carry in your pocket, isn't it? What you toy with when you're restless or nervous?"

He nodded, and the rift between us deepened.

"Couldn't be a silver dollar or a rabbit's foot, huh? Is there anything else binding you to your ex-wife?"

"No."

I turned to him. "No other stray animals or little

charms—trinkets hidden away in some cookie jar, maybe?"

He winced, dropping his gaze to the shabby scrap of leather. "No. There's nothing else."

I stood and went for the robe in my closet. I shrugged into it, tying the belt around my waist, needing the support for what I was about to say. "Thank you for finally being honest with me. As crummy as I feel right now, at least I have the truth."

"Goldie—"

I stopped him with a hand in the air then walked over to the window and pushed back the curtains. I couldn't hide any longer. As much as I wanted to leave his ex-wife and the rest of their past outside—and keep Max to myself—I knew it was a ridiculous notion. *It's downright destructive to my sanity.*

I took a few deep breaths to clear my head, then spoke without looking at him. "I need to be alone. I think it'd be best if we didn't see each other for a while. Besides, your workload has just doubled with the university proposal...and I'm headed home for a few weeks."

"I didn't know that." He sat up a little taller.

His words felt hollow and cold in my ears. *Yeah, well neither did I until thirty seconds ago. Screw Ace's irrigation redesign project. I want my mom.*

"Well, now you do." I swiped my hand across my eyes to dry them, then turned. "This is a lot, Max. I thought I could handle things with you and your ex-wife and your history...but right now I'm not so sure. I don't know how I feel. I don't think you do either."

"I've made mistakes, I know that. I'm sorry I didn't tell you sooner." He stood and closed the space between us.

I took a step backward, capturing his gaze. "Why didn't you tell me this the other night—when you dumped the rest of your shit on me?"

"I don't know. I guess I wasn't thinking about it."

Seriously...?

"And for the record, I disagree. I don't think pulling back is going to help us work through this. But I'm going to give you what you want, Goldie. You're all that matters to me."

My knees trembled, and I clutched the lapels of my robe. My stomach was bungee jumping off a cliff, and sadly, the sinking dive had nothing to do with the stomach bug. I closed my eyes, wishing I could put our memories on repeat in my mind and never wake up. I was silently screaming for Max to gather me in his arms and hold me until this horrible storm passed.

I swayed, and he caught me by the elbows. *And what did I say?* "Right...I'll need to think on that one."

Max moved suddenly, grabbing the bracelet and sliding the beads off the strip of leather. He cupped them in his hands, walked out the door of my apartment, and threw them across the parking lot. When he returned, he stuffed the frayed leather strip into the garbage disposal, turned on the water, and ground it to smithereens. He turned around, leaned back against the counter, and crossed his arms.

I pulled the belt on my robe tighter, hugging my arms around my middle. My body knew Max and I were great together, but in the past fifteen minutes, my mind had tallied a half dozen reasons we couldn't last. *Ashley, Ashley, Ashley, Ashley, Ashley...oh yeah, and Ashley.* And to punctuate this war raging inside me, my heart clung to one unmistakable, undeniable truth. *I love you, Max.*

His expression was all quiet concentration, the corners of his mouth tight. He cleared his throat. "I can't make you love me. Hell, *I* don't even love me. But for what it's worth, I'm in love with you, Goldie. I've known it for some time, but I didn't have the guts to tell you. Leave if you have to but I'm not going anywhere. I'm going to wait for you, for as long as you need." He came to me and whispered in my ear. "To give me—*us*—another chance." Then, he pivoted and walked out of my apartment.

****

After showering and packing my suitcase, I gathered my wits and phoned Ethan. I spoke honestly, but with reserve.

"I know I just told you about the project yesterday. I can't thank you enough for understanding." I listened while Ethan reassured me it was no problem, and I felt the knot in my throat loosen.

When I shared Ace's bank loan approval and timeline, Ethan's voice lifted. "As I said before, this is a project CDD will want to bid on. If you can manage to get the initial assessment and specs to me before the July fourth holiday—and work remotely on our other commitments while you're there—then take all the time you need."

I thanked him again and was headed home to Three Creeks within the hour. One hundred thirty miles and one rest area later, my feet landed on the soil I'd known my whole life.

I spent the next couple weeks working with Ace and living a virtually Max-less existence. After coming in from Raleigh for the July fourth weekend, my sister, Prim, took an extra week of vacation from the hospital just to be close to me.

Except for a handful of cryptic texts, Max and I didn't talk. I winced, remembering his text about how my retired neighbor—the one who was coming over to feed my fish every other day—had called him to report fire ants were taking over my patio, and then another one explaining how maintenance had put out bait to kill what she called "the little buggers."

Why does my neighbor even have his number...?

As if reading my mind, Max texted he'd stopped by to see her, giving her his number in case anything happened at my apartment while I was gone. After I thanked him, he replied with a sweet, *—I've got you, Peach.—*

I slowly fell into a routine at home, jogging around the farm with Prim before breakfast, working on CDD projects during the day, then helping Mom with her flower shop and garden until supper. My family was cathartic.

Mom. She wore a chambray shirt, work jeans, and garden gloves every day, and was my kindred spirit, all healthy and earth loving.

Prim. She possessed a natural kind of grace—neither learned nor overly polished—and lifted my spirits with simple things like braiding my hair and baking us bran muffins.

And Ace...? Well, he stayed close without hovering, but the way he grumbled under his breath sometimes made me think he longed for the days when all I needed was the threat of his fists against the likes of Kyle Peterson.

This morning, I didn't get past the front gate on our run before I was hunched over at the waist, puking into a row of nandina bushes. Prim led me back to the house where I slid into a chair at the kitchen table. I managed to smile when she brought over saltines and a sparkling water.

My sister took the chair beside me, lifting a questioning brow while she checked my pulse. She released my wrist, a line creasing her brow. "This is the second time this week. What gives?"

I took a long swallow of my drink, letting the carbonation settle my insides. "I had the stomach flu a couple weeks ago. I swear, I haven't been right since." I lowered my head to the table, nibbling sideways on a cracker.

Prim touched my brow. "No fever. But we ate the same supper last night, and I feel fine."

"Yeah, Max never got sick either."

She leaned forward, elbows on the table. "You fell asleep on the sofa yesterday afternoon."

I polished off the cracker and reached for another, chewing quietly. Suddenly a tiny little alarm tripped in my brain. I bolted upright, chin gaping, and Prim watched me, giving voice to my thoughts.

"Is it possible you're—"

I shook my head, not in denial but confusion, and my hands hovered over my belly. "No way," I blurted, then revised with a shaky, "God, probably not?"

"Sweetie, I asked if it's possible, not probable. And since I know you two have been having sex, I'd say it's a definite...*possibility*. Are you late?"

I needed a moment of space to sift through her question. My period came the week before the Shembery trip. Then everything started happening with Max so quickly. *But we use protection all the time.* My weekly planner was sharp in my thoughts. *Shit, I don't remember buying tampons last month.*

"But can't your cycle get a little off when you first go on the pill?" I countered.

Prim frowned. "I know it says you're covered in like a week, but I believe in using back up for like a month or so. Just to be safe."

"We did." As if I needed proof, I dashed to my bedroom, grabbed the near-empty box, and came back, waving it in the air. "We used condoms. Lots and lots of them!"

She scooted her chair closer, draping an arm over my shoulder. "Hey, breathe please. Slowly. In…out." As I complied, Prim took the box, her gaze skimming the print on the side of the box.

"Premium protection, my ass," I scoffed between breaths.

She nudged my shoulder, biting her bottom lip. "Um, you might want to read this. Looks like you two weren't just fighting the odds with the pill and stomach flu." She held the box for me. "These things have expiration dates, you know."

"But I got them right before the trip. I swear it!"

Prim blew out a weighty sigh, shrugging. "Well, I guess the drugstore employees didn't cycle through their stock because this box definitely got overlooked."

"Well, that should be illegal. This kind of screwup can change people's lives…forever!" My fingers drifted to my necklace, details resurfacing about making love with Max after he clasped it around my neck. I'd said, *I've never seen anything more beautiful.*

And he'd replied, *I have. And I'm looking right at her.*

I grabbed my sister's arm. "Holy shit! We didn't use one the night before I got sick."

"You said it yourself, honey. You barfed up everything but your stomach lining—that probably means the pill, too." She kissed me on the forehead, whispering softly, "But the reasons don't really matter. You can get pregnant even when you're careful."

I fell into my sister's arms, quiet sobs raking my shoulders. "Oh, God, Prim. What am I going to do…?"

"You're not going to do anything. But *we* are."

I pulled back, startled. In that moment, I was in the air between two trapezes, my sister's words the safety net below me. A shiver ran up my spine, and my gut clenched. I covered my mouth and rushed to the bathroom.

It took me a few minutes to empty the rest of my stomach, freshen my breath with mouthwash, and splash water over my face. I patted my cheeks with a hand towel. *God, is this what the next nine months are going to be like?* I looked in the mirror, cupping my heavy breasts. *I'm going to need a body harness before this is over.* Because I was pregnant. I knew it. And my life would never be the same.

I returned to the kitchen and announced, "I'm pregnant, Prim. I know it."

"First of all, we're not going to panic. And second, we're going to get a bunch of pregnancy tests, so we'll know what we're dealing with."

"When they're all positive, I'll tell you what we'll be dealing with. A whole lot of heartache." And if I truly owned it, a heavy dose of humiliation, too. I could hear the rumor mill humming. *Promising young engineer loses her heart to the man everyone—except* Goldie—*knows is emotionally unavailable.*

It wasn't like I didn't want children. I did…and I wanted them with Max. *But now? Like this? Really, God?*

I was a raging bundle of pregnancy hormones, soon to be amped up on prenatal vitamins. Stretch marks and bladder leaks loomed ahead. Sleepless nights and solo visits to the obstetrician—and later the pediatrician—invaded my thoughts.

But would I be alone?

Sure, Sofia said Max wanted a family, and he was great with Jack's children, but he hadn't talked to me about kids. He'd only said he loved me once, and that was in the heat of the moment. This baby bomb would come at him—and everyone I cared about—out of left field.

I shook my head. "Could this be any worse? How can I keep my job when everyone finds out? And what will Mom think? And Max, he's gonna freak—"

"Goldie. Get a grip, okay? Everyone knows you two are in a relationship."

"Or were?" I bit into my bottom lip. "They also know I'm hopelessly in love with him."

"Which is not necessarily a bad thing." She cupped my cheeks in her hands, grinning. "Now, stop catastrophizing and get your butt in gear. We're going to the drugstore."

Chapter Twenty-Three

Wednesday, July 14th 9:22 p.m.
Max

I wasn't sure how long I'd been hunched over my laptop, but if the throbbing in my shoulders was any indication, it'd been too damn long. I pushed away from my desk, rolling backward in my chair and lifting my arms in a stretch. The hallways were silent, the drone of the vacuum having ceased hours ago with the exit of the cleaning service. The spreadsheet on my laptop glared at me, mocking me for being at the office at such an ungodly hour.

I pulled my Swiss army knife from my pocket, rubbing my thumb over the smooth red casing and faded emblem. At our last counseling session, Andy had encouraged me to find a replacement for the old leather band. I went straight home and dug out the cigar box from my bottom dresser drawer. Inside, alongside my grandpa's brass ashtray, a two-dollar bill, and my first driver's license, I found my trusty knife. As I fanned out the nail file and scissors, I remembered carrying it with me everywhere—until Ashley made the bracelet and it took the coveted place in my pocket.

I folded the pieces back inside the knife and put it on my desk. I spun it around like a top before covering it with my palm. With a sigh, I dropped the knife back in my pocket. *Wish I'd chosen you over that leather strap a long time ago.* I didn't miss it any more than I missed Ashley. *I only miss Peach.*

Off in the distance, I heard the faint click of the microwave oven door followed by a sequence of beeps. *What the...?* I shook my head when a whirlwind of popping sounds lifted in the air. As steady feet approached some moments later, I stood with my hands on my hips.

Standing in the doorway, Dad's gaze met mine, and he held out a bag of popcorn like a peace pipe. "Should I have brought you supper?" he asked, cocking his head thoughtfully. "Yes, especially since your mother fixed a nice to-go box for you."

"Then where is it?"

He flashed me a sheepish look. "On the corner of the island...right where she left it. Didn't even realize I'd forgotten the damn thing until I pulled into the parking lot."

I laughed, imagining Mom's expression of loving bewilderment once she spotted the container on the counter. "You know she's going to give you hell, right?"

"Yeah, she'll start talking to me again about those memory supplements."

"You know she's never met a vitamin she didn't like." The moment the words left my mouth, I thought of Goldie. *And her leafy greens...and her miraculous cinnamon.*

Dad offered the bag of popcorn in consolation. "It's not her pork tenderloin and apple cobbler, but it'll keep you from starving."

With a nod, I took it and gestured for him to sit down. He took the chair across from my desk, leaning back and folding his arms across his chest.

I ripped open the bag, releasing the steam, and shrugged one shoulder. "Eh, it's nothing new. I'm used to fending for myself."

I glanced over at my dad, his frown at my offhand comment reminding me how raw my divorce still was to my family. I shoveled popcorn in my mouth, thinking nothing sucked more than being the oldest of three kids and the one everybody fussed over. Did they actually think I hadn't noticed their sidestepping last December, like I couldn't manage a decent 'plus-one' for my cousin's wedding? Or that the mail-order steak subscription they gave me for my birthday was over-the-top considering I'd divorced Ashley, not my housekeeper?

I shook my head, conceding that while I might go home to an empty house, my housekeeper made sure there was more than beer and ketchup in the refrigerator. *Things like scallops and fresh vegetables in a bowl on the counter.* I thought of Goldie and avocados, then landing on the *Fifty Ways* I'd fucked up our relationship, pushed out a painful breath.

Dad cleared his throat, his gaze dark. "You're driving too hard, Son. You're exhausted. I'd just like to see you enjoying yourself more after the year you've had."

For fuck's sake, wasn't I doing that? Until I went and freaked out my girlfriend? I wanted to build a home with Goldie, with her as my wife and our kids leaving behind those annoying soap rings in the bathtub. If it didn't hurt so bad, I'd admit the years I wasted in a broken-record marriage made me want the white picket fence a little *too* much.

Knowing my dad had my best interests at heart, I

forced a smile, trying to show—for like the ninetieth time—I was indeed *fine*.

"Hey. I'm fine, Dad. Really. *Fine*."

He shook his head dismissively. "No, you're not. Otherwise you wouldn't be holed up here in your office at all hours of the night. Don't you think it's about time you go after Goldie?"

I shoved the bag of popcorn aside, pushed out of my chair, and walked over to the mini fridge. As I reached for a water, I couldn't deny his question was the same one that'd been bouncing around in my head since she left. *Nineteen days and about a dozen hours ago, if I'm counting...which clearly I am.*

I took a few long swallows, wiping my mouth with the back of my hand, and thought back to last night. What I'd begun to realize, while staring at a dark TV screen during yet another sleepless night, was the loss of intimacy in my marriage—sacrificed somewhere between our initial vows and eventual irreconcilable differences—had triggered a chain reaction. Ashley and I relied on shortcuts in our relationship, blaming our professional obligations when hours turned to days without so much as a peck on the lips. As a result, our lackluster love life drove us deeper into work, each finding successes there while our marriage withered.

If we'd started our life together as a neatly woven scarf, the rips and snags along the way had taken their toll. Shortcuts led to a complacent unintentional relationship, unraveling at the seams.

Dad coughed, drawing my attention. "Well, if you can't go after her...yet," he said, crossing one leg over the other, "can you at least put some distance between you and the office?"

"Uh, I'm here because this is where the work gets done," I said, deadpanning.

"You have mobility, Max. Hotspots, VPNs, wireless…"

Says the guy who signs off on paper expense reports. I turned to face him, leaning my hip against the desk. "I need to focus. I do my best work here." I paused long enough to capture his gaze. "I want the university deal. It's been a long time coming. And to get it, everything has to be right."

"Yep, I used to tell myself the same thing." He scratched his jaw, a day's worth of stubble casting a shadow over his face. "Until I learned better."

A dry crackle hung at the back of my throat, so I pulled on my water bottle, baffled as to where this conversation was headed.

"I used to keep a ledger of all our accounts—detailed entries about billable hours, designs, specs, cost-benefits. You name it, I tracked it." He raised an eyebrow. "You've probably got some kick-ass spreadsheet just like it."

I glanced at my laptop. *Damn right, I do.*

"I made the ledger to hold myself accountable—to learn from my mistakes—so when I screwed something up, I could look back. Figure out where I went wrong."

"Bet that rarely happened."

He chuckled. "Oh, but it did. More often than I'd like to admit. You know, it's time I let you in on a little secret." He shifted forward in his chair, elbows resting on his knees. "You want to know the one thing I learned from looking back at my ledger?"

I nodded like when I was a kid, and he was my batting coach.

"The jobs where I logged the most hours away from home always turned out to be the least rewarding. It's like God had to take a hammer to my head to get me to understand the purpose behind balancing my work and my family."

Intrigued, I hopped onto my desk, listening while my dad spun his tale about CDD. I'd interned at the company since prep school, spending my summer breaks disaggregating data and traipsing behind him at work sites. I had no recollection of these time-sucking clients and their projects, and I told him as much.

"What I'm talking about happened early on, while you and James were little. I soon realized failure at work was a cake walk compared to how I felt when I let your mother down," Dad said, voice trailing off. "What I'm trying to say is don't lose sight of yourself, Son, and what's truly important in life."

At that, I slid off my desk, finished my water, and tossed the bottle in the recycling can. A slow current of defensiveness pulsed through my veins. I didn't need reminding how Bedrock James had his shit together, and Limestone Max didn't.

"Right. Right." My hands found their way to my hair, pulling straight through to the ends. "Look, I really have let Ashley go. And even though it doesn't look like it sometimes, I'm moving on…I hope somehow…with Goldie." As uncertainty pierced my thoughts, I swung back into my trusty lane. "But in the meantime, this bid is due tomorrow, which means I'm submitting it by midnight. Tonight."

"And what about tomorrow?"

I barked out a laugh, shrugging my shoulders. "Jesus, Dad. Take your pick. I've got my own backlog, plus there are things I'm working on with James so he can go out with Anna when the baby comes." I stepped backward, engulfed with a bitterness I'd probably never be in my brother's shoes—never be a father. The realization sucked out what little warmth was left inside me. "Or I don't know, maybe you'll find some other mess for me to fix tomorrow. You say I'm your best closer." I glared at my dad. "But I think we both know I'm behind in the count with my life."

Dad thundered to his feet, sending his chair skidding backward. "Damn it, Max. You're not listening."

I gazed at him and saw the trademark Corda fire and determination in his gray eyes. But his shoulders, once a rock-solid place for me to perch as a child, had softened with age. It was impossible to miss the vein in his brow—exactly like mine—that throbbed whenever he got riled up. And underneath everything, what else did Myles Corda have…? *Balls of fucking steel.*

I didn't know what stoked my anger, but it needed to get out.

"No. Please. I *am* listening." I reached for his arms, gripping them tight. "Tell me how to let go, okay? Will you do that? Because the way I see it, all I've got going for me is this company. Success breeds success, Dad. And failure?" I said, stiffly. "Just breeds more failure."

The silence that followed was stunned, painful. I blinked a few times before letting my hands fall to my sides. I flexed my fingers to keep them from curling into fists. My brain ached, and my heart stung.

As my knees buckled, Dad caught me. He wrapped me in the blanket of his arms, hugging me, supporting me.

Saving me.

"Come here, Son," he whispered over my ear, squeezing me tight against his chest. "Come here. I've got you."

With those three simple words, I caved, surrendering to the pull of his voice and strength of his embrace. I'd been closed tight as an abandoned house for a long time, boards nailed into the windows sealing out the sunlight and fresh air. I needed to let him inside, let him help me silence my fear of failure…for good.

Chapter Twenty-Four

Thursday, July 15th 9:05 a.m.
Goldie

I ate a protein yogurt with granola before going on my walk, and it seemed to agree with me. Back at the house, waiting for my laptop to wake up, I scrolled through my texts. As the teakettle whistled in the kitchen, I grabbed my things and headed in that direction.

I slid into a chair at the table, and Mom flashed me a smile. Everything I knew about motherhood I learned from her or my grandmothers. As I ticked off their superhuman gifts in my head—from untangling necklaces to actually making an edible meal with only three ingredients—I tried not to feel intimidated.

Mom placed two cups on the table and sat beside me. "Try this lemon, ginger, and honey tea. I bet my grandbaby will approve."

I took a sip, hesitated, then set the cup on the table. I glanced at my mom, mouth opening and shutting a couple times. "I'm sorry, Mom. I-I know this is not happening the way it's supposed to."

" 'Supposed to' isn't you. It never has been."

"Billie and Mark have given you a proper grandchild." Before she could protest, I shook my head, apologetically. "Please don't think bad of me. I know I'm single, but I'm smart and capable of taking care of myself and this child. I have money saved up, too." I rubbed my belly. "And besides, I'm already so in love with this little peanut, I hardly know what to do with myself."

Mom chuckled. "First of all, I could never feel anything but love and pride in you, and you know it. I'll love this grandchild the same as the one I already have—with all my heart. You'd make an amazing single mom, but somehow I don't think that's in the cards for you." She touched my cheek with the back of her hand. "Have you decided when you're going to talk to Max?"

My heart twisted. I hadn't decided…but I needed to soon. Every day I left him in the dark felt like a ticking bomb. Knowing I needed to work my way out of my head, but not quite ready to do it, I replied with a feeble, "Not exactly."

My mom was a unique blend of pragmatic mother of six and romantic English teacher, a firm believer there was little either peppermint antacid or a sonnet couldn't cure. With both elbows propped on the table, she held her cup in her hands, blowing over the steam.

"I love you, and I believe you deserve time to think things through, but honey…" Mom said, the hitch in her voice unmistakable, "Max needs to know what's going on. If you don't tell him soon, aren't you guilty of holding back? The same way he did with you?" When I didn't answer, she reached out to touch my arm. "I guess what I'm asking is what do you hope to gain by putting this off?"

Shoot, it looked like she was doling out the peppermint stuff. *But I want the lovey-dovey poetry.* I sighed, knowing the truth of my predicament lurked somewhere between the two extremes.

I wiggled around in my chair. Was I keeping the pregnancy from Max because I wanted to handle all of this on my own? *Not a chance.* Or was I camped out at home because I was afraid my fantasy might not come true? The one where I told him about our baby, and he magically slipped a ring on my finger and whisked us away to some secluded wedding destination?

Yeah, that's more like it.

"Goldie…?"

I groaned into my teacup. "Ugh, Mom."

She set her cup down, folding her hands in her lap and watching me for a few long moments. Under her gaze, the weight pressing on my heart quadrupled. My reluctance to talk to Max wasn't about gaining something. It was about losing *everything.*

I turned to Mom and, reading the crinkle on her brow as a green light, unloaded a string of fears, insecurities, and general chaotic tendencies on her. She listened until I finally dropped my head, and my ranting ceased.

Mom clasped my hand in hers. "You're obsessing, Goldie. You've worked this thing up so much you're losing sight of what is fundamentally important. You and Max have created a little life here, and it's growing inside you as we speak. Rather than expecting a fairy tale, maybe you could try leaning into the truth."

"But he hasn't been in touch with me for weeks. Well, except for a couple of lame texts."

"But you asked him to leave you alone, right?"

"Well, but not for forever," I countered.

"He's been doing what you asked." Her words struck a chord inside me, and I felt my mouth twisting into a frown. "I think you miss him…and I also think you're sick of not knowing what your future holds. May I ask you something?"

I nodded.

"Are you absolutely sure you're in love with Max? I don't know, maybe you got all caught up in the idea of love, but now you're not so sure about the man and his history."

Okay, so Pragmatic Mom just crossed a red line.

"How can you even say such a thing? I know we haven't been together forever like you and Dad were…or Billie and Mark." With a huff, I crossed my arms on the table. "But I don't need years to figure out I love Max. He's brilliant, and so caring and kind. I love how he protects his family, how his heart still allows him to care about his ex-wife when she's grieving."

I pushed back from the table and continued. "It's his good heart that struggled to let go of the bracelet. But he did let it go, Mom. He destroyed the thing right in front of me. I love him *because* of his giant, amazing, forgiving heart. I don't need our initials carved into the tree trunk by the creek to know what I feel for him is real, *truth and dare* love."

Mom smirked.

Then it all made sense. *How could I forget she's Sneaky Mom, too?* "How do you do it?"

She grinned over the rim of her cup. "I have no idea what you're talking about."

"You sort out hearts even better than mismatched socks. Thank you for reminding me what I've got—how I'm enough, and he's enough, and together we're more than enough."

"I'm glad you see that now, but hey, don't you mean Truth *or* Dare?"

"Nope," I said, climbing out of my chair and going in for a hug. "That's not the way I'm going to play this."

Mom pressed a kiss to my temple. "I love you, Goldie. Everything's going to work out—I feel it in my heart."

Her words weren't lost on me, and I dashed out of the kitchen, exhilaration pumping through my veins for the first time in weeks. When I first met Max, the idea of talking to him petrified me. He was this polished professional, complete with clean fingernails and a smile bordering on sinful. But after watching him traipse through the stormwater drainage areas at Shembery Isle and later joke about the stains on his khakis, I realized he wasn't stiff at all. *He's incredibly real.*

I smiled, Sofia's words hovering at the edges of my mind. Max was a solid, straight-arrow kind of guy—no connector of someone else's random dots—and a maker of masterpieces. I touched my tummy, a secret smile tugging at my lips. After the shock wears off, Max will be as thrilled about our little masterpiece as me…maybe even more so.

As I stepped into the shower, I thought back to the baseball game and the evening we spent with Jack's children. Instead of eyes brimming with tears for their brother, Nate and Janie had been all sing-along songs and giggles with Max. I turned the nozzle to rain shower, my mind relaxing with the memory of how he wore Janie's cheese goatee and held Nate snugly on his lap. *He's going to be an amazing father.*

I worked the shampoo through my hair, mustering my courage. While seeing Max didn't scare me anymore, one thing did weigh heavy on my heart. Love was love, but a baby was…well…what I said to Mom. *An honest-to-goodness Truth* and *Dare.*

Chapter Twenty-Five

Thursday, July 15th 11:45 a.m.
Max
"What color are Goldie's eyes?"

I stood on the other side of an oak desk, watching Ace Vreeland rummage through a drawer. I kept my gaze on him, reading him, imagining myself in his shoes. I'd lost count of the number of questions he asked, but it didn't matter. I'd answer a hundred of them because I knew the path to Goldie went through her oldest brother.

In a matter of seconds, Ace found what he was looking for—a box of toothpicks—and slid one between his teeth. It bobbed up and down as he asked, "Need me to repeat the question, Corda?"

I met his gaze. "Blue. A beautiful clear lake blue."

"Zodiac?"

"Aries." I was silent for a moment, then added, "In case you're wondering, I'm a Virgo."

Ace grunted, crossing his arms over his chest. "Bet you don't know her full name."

It was a good thing I understood protective instincts because in spite of the interrogation, I saw a bit of myself in Ace. The man owned his responsibilities and put family first—especially his sisters. I could say without hesitation I'd do the same and hammer any guy who'd messed with my sister's heart. I hooked my hands behind my back and answered, "Goldenrod Mayes Vreeland."

He pointed his toothpick in my direction. "Does she like coffee or tea for breakfast?"

"Breakfast?" I took a slow breath, choosing my words carefully. "Then I guess you know Goldie and I have become quite…close."

As the word and all its implications hung in the air between us, Ace grumbled something under his breath. He tossed the toothpick in the trashcan and met my gaze. "Yeah. I know. I already talked to my sister, and as much as I hate thinking about her like that with *any* guy, I'm damn well going to make sure he's not a dickweed. So, can you answer the question?"

I stood tall and held my ground. "No coffee. She likes green tea with fresh lemon and raw unfiltered honey with breakfast."

Ace chewed on the inside of his cheek for a couple agonizing moments then gestured to the chair across from his desk.

"If I may," I asked, sitting and giving him a deferential look, "why don't I tell you what I've learned about your sister over the past few months? Then you can decide if you want to kick my ass back to Charlotte."

He let out an unguarded chuckle, giving me hope the scales might be tipping my way.

I rested my elbows on the arms of the chair, hands clasped together. "Well, for one thing, since Goldie can't have a dog in her apartment, she has a saltwater aquarium. She cares about things other than herself and swears her fish happy-swim when she comes near them."

Ace steepled his hands under his chin, and I cleared my throat. "Your sister is beautiful, and yes, she makes heads turn. But it's her spontaneity and honesty that capture imaginations. Mine most of all."

I leaned forward in my chair. "She loves her family and is proud of her heritage, but I think she's the toughest Vreeland of them all. She inspires everyone with her brilliant mind and spirit. She just...sparkles." My throat got a little tight, but I forged ahead. "Goldie. Christ, she's everything to me."

I rose to my feet, a rush of possessiveness coursing through my veins, and stared down at Ace. "In case you can't tell, I'm in love with your sister. I know you almost decked Kyle Peterson for harassing her when they were kids. Hell, you probably want to punch me right now, and you can if that will make things better between us. But I can tell you I'm not going anywhere. If Goldie will have me, I'll love her for the rest of my life."

I took a deep breath and pulled the ring box out of my pocket. I lifted the lid, revealing the emerald-cut diamond engagement ring I'd ordered from Andersen's weeks ago, and showed it to Ace. "I'm going to ask your sister to marry me, Mr. Vreeland. I'd really like to do it with your blessing."

As Ace stared at the ring and me, tension tugged at my neck. I clocked my breathing, in and out...in and out. Though a frown creased his brow, it only steeled my resolve. *Give me your best shot, Ace.* While I'd made a shit ton of mistakes in my life, I knew I wasn't a failure. I loved Goldie and nothing—not even her brother—would stop me from asking her to be my wife.

Ace turned and picked up the family photo from the corner of his desk. He cocked his head as if looking for something new in the familiar faces. He sliced his gaze at me. "She actually told you about Kyle?"

I nodded. "And I don't mind telling you I wanted to kick his ass."

Of course, he didn't respond. Not even a grunt. Instead, he narrowed his eyes and pointed to the photo in his hand.

"I want you to take a good long look at this, Corda. All three of my sisters are amazing women, and I'd protect them with my life. But Goldie," he said, the tenor of his voice softening, "she's got a place in my heart all to herself." He put the photo back in its place and came around his desk. He stopped two feet in front of me, hands on his hips. "I only threatened to beat the shit out of that kid a long time ago, but with you...? I'll absolutely do it if you hurt her any more than you already have. You can count on it."

His vow nailed me in my heart. I wasn't used to feeling this out of my depth, but then I'd never screwed up so badly as I had with Goldie. "Understood."

He scratched his head. "And as much as I'd like to send you packing, this is Goldie's decision. Come on, I'll take you to the house." He paused, a smile in his eyes, but his mouth set in something more thoughtful. "And you can call me Ace."

****

I stopped at Goldie's bedroom door. The knuckles in my fist were poised for knocking, but my fingertips felt like they had little lead weights inside them. Suddenly a quick calculation flickered through my head...a semester in college lasted longer than the few months I'd been with Goldie. *How is that even possible...?*

I shook off the thought, completely certain in my heart I'd known her all my life. The precious years ahead of us were all that mattered to me. I rolled my shoulders, tilting my head from side to side, then knocked on the door.

The music that'd been playing in her room went silent. I heard light feet shuffling across the floor, then Goldie swung open the door and on a winded breath said, "Finally, I texted you like—"

"Hi." The word rolled off my tongue, surprisingly steady given the tornado of nerves in my gut. Though this had never been a break-up in my mind, a sliver of doubt lingered in my head our separation might have meant that to her.

Goldie sucked in her breath, fingers covering her mouth. "Max…?"

God, how I wished my lips were where her fingers were, but instinct told me to tread carefully. I wanted to kiss her, but I wanted *her* kiss even more. I'd still give her space if she needed it, but I couldn't take any more of this long distance crap.

I was ready to label every feeling in my heart.

I wasn't opposed to begging.

And I was absolutely never letting go of what we had without a fight.

"Hello, Peach."

****

Goldie

I slapped my hand over my mouth, leaning against my bedroom door to keep from toppling into Max. The shock of seeing him reminded me there's something pure and unexpected about love. It defies reason and is too complex for even search engine analytics. It doesn't care one whit about likes or follows or trends on social media. Love is singular, elusive, continuously sought-after, and the only thing in this world truly worth fighting for.

When he called me Peach, the hoarse affection in his

voice made my heart clinch. I tilted my head to one side, noting how his hair lacked its usual shine and his cheekbones had a darker, edgier look. I judged the stubble on his jaw to be a good day and a half's growth, begging the question of how he'd spent the past thirty-six hours. *Working, not sleeping, not eating…?* I touched my forehead, wondering if he noticed my stress pimples, then blinked, guessing my eyes were cloudy from some sleep deprivation of my own. My gaze fell to my belly then lifted to his face.

"Surprise much, Mr. Corda?"

"Oddly enough, no, Ms. Vreeland. Most people find me predictable…and a little too stuck in my thoughts."

I rested my head against the door and breathed a sigh. How had I actually turned away from Max, casting aside the warmth of his smile for an endless string of cloudy days? Oh, I'd had some lofty ideas about simpler relationships and baggage-less guys, but my logic sounded more like fortune cookie ramblings now.

God had blessed Max with a deeply considerate soul and high-density heart, but Ashley no longer ruled either of them. He'd given me the truth—the phone conversation about Merry's death, the charm he hoped would ease his ex-wife's grief, and the destruction of the childhood bracelet—and I let pride and fear skew my common sense.

Yet I couldn't consider our separation a complete waste. Without it, I wouldn't have discovered how much I missed the way he hooked his chin over my shoulder while I brushed my teeth before bed. And I'd have never realized how I longed for that perfect scent of cotton and sandalwood in his shirt. I breathed in, wanting to bury my face between his collar and neck…so I did.

Steadfast, he enfolded me in his arms, the movement sending a tide of happiness washing through my body. *This is what matters...Max and me and baby Corda.*

I listened to the rapid thumps of his heart beneath my ear. *He's as nervous as I am.* Suddenly, I understood without the separation, I couldn't have put pride and fear in their proper place. Real life was happiness raining down on you but having the smarts to dig your heels in the ground when you needed to ride out the storms.

I pressed my lips to his Adam's apple, speaking against his skin. "I kind of like the thinking that goes on behind your handsome face."

Max released a shuddering breath. "That's good to know because I have a few things to tell you."

The old me would have tensed at his declaration. *But not the reconditioned me.*

Max lowered his arms and took a step backward. "I love you, Goldenrod Mayes Vreeland, and that's never ever going to change. I promise to be your equal, honest, and supportive partner in life. I'll never put anything before us—not work, not money, or any other obligations. My goal is to find personal and professional balance for the rest of my life...with you." A crease formed on his brow, and he blew out a breath. "Do you think you could share your life with me even though I'm pretty sure I'll mess up in the future? I promise it won't ever be because of lies or manipulation though. Only small stupid stuff."

I felt my heart expanding in my chest. "Like when you put the toilet paper on backward?" I asked, tease-whispering.

"That's neither small nor stupid. You're the one putting the roll on wrong. Everyone knows the sheet should roll off the top."

I thought about that for a moment. "Like the flat sheet goes on top of a bed?"

He kissed me on the nose. "Exactly. I knew I loved you for more than your body," he added, a grin reaching his eyes. "Can you forgive my mistakes and spend forever with me despite the occasional mess?"

"Before I give you my answer, how do you feel about cleaning up other people's messes?"

I could practically hear the cogs in his brain turning. "Purposeful or accidental?"

As my mind filled with images of poop-filled diapers, spit-up towels, and juice stains on vintage wool rugs, I shook my head. "More the natural, unavoidable kind."

"You know my thoughts on nature's 'mess is best.' " Max pulled back, his gaze scanning my expression like he was hunting for a four-leaf clover. I caught myself biting my lip and quickly released it.

"You want to tell me something, Peach," he said without a hint of question in his tone.

"Yes, I do." I summoned the bravest breath I could and spit out the words. "Truth and Dare, Max." When he drew his brows down, I stood a little taller. "That's right. You heard me, Truth *and* Dare."

He scratched his chin. "Okay...you've got my attention. Truth."

"Okay, truth. I love you, too, Maxwell Lynd Corda. I'm sure you've known that for a while. But I can't help it—I don't *want* to help it—because you're everything to me."

A look of relief washed over his face, and he followed it with a gentle question. "And dare...?"

I let those two words sink in. Glancing down at my outfit—a racer-back tank top and leggings—I tried to visualize my curves in nine months. I crossed my arms over my chest. *God, my boobs will need their own zip code before this is all over.* My gaze wandered over his leather loafers, then lifted higher to his jeans. The shade matched the man...*true damn blue.* A ripple of nausea rushed through my stomach, and I reached for him. Without a word, he led me to my bed and kneeled beside me.

"This is better anyway," Max said so softly I bet he thought I didn't hear him. As he reached inside his pocket, my heart tripped a beat. He rubbed his thumb over my chin. "We don't need your dare 'cause I'm proposing the greatest one of all." In his other hand, he held a beautiful emerald-cut diamond ring. "Will you marry me, Goldie? You name the date, the time, the place—anything you want. Just please say you'll be my wife, and I'll spend the rest of my life loving you."

Emotion swelled in my chest, a feeling so strong it rushed out into every part of my body. Everything instantly came into focus, full circle.

"Yes. I will absolutely marry you," I said, my head bobbing. "Nothing would make me happier. I love you so much!"

Max scooped me into his arms, taking my place on the bed and cradling me in his lap. He kissed me with abandon, and the weeks apart melted away in our shared warmth. I was starved for him, needing the intimacy of his lips, the light nipping of his teeth. I protested when his mouth left mine to skate light kisses over my cheek.

"Please tell me these are tears of joy."

"They are." I laughed a little, wiping my eyes. *Most*

likely caused by pregnancy hormones.

"Doesn't matter. I hate seeing you cry, Peach."

"I think you'd better get used to it. They say tears come with the territory." Reading the question in his eyes, I slid off his lap. "Yeah, so about my dare." I closed my eyes, took a deep breath, and opened them. "I'm pregnant, Max."

****

Max

I dragged my hands through my hair and hooked them behind my neck, lifting my face heavenward. Did Goldie just say she was…pregnant?

Sweet.

Holy.

God.

Something this wonderful, this unforeseen, didn't just happen to a man like me. I measured things in life, and with my workaholic tendencies no longer tipping the scale, I felt the balance was reasonably intact. I whooshed out a breath, incredulous Goldie and I had created a life together…through our love. How do you respond to your soulmate and to God for giving you the greatest blessing in life?

I'm definitely going to need a bigger scale.

"Max…? You're scaring me. Say something."

I met her gaze, searching her indigo eyes. Finding no words equal to my elation, I dropped to my knees, wrapping my arms around her waist and pressing my face against her belly. I slid her tank top up and kissed her there, over and over. With my eyes closed, I imagined the tiny life inside her and how it would grow into this amazing little person. As Goldie slid her hands through my hair, rubbing her fingers in gentle circles, I hugged her closer.

In time, I lifted my head, comforted when I found her gazing at me. In a raspy voice full of conviction, I said, "That's one hell of a Truth and Dare. I love you, Peach. I've never felt so happy, so blessed, as I do right now."

Goldie cupped my cheeks in her hands. "Glad you liked it. And I love you, too."

A string of questions flooded through my head. "When did you—how long—?"

She pressed her finger to my lips, then helped me to my feet. I held her hand, and we sat together, thigh against thigh, while she shared the events of the past weeks. I nodded, remembering the night we'd forgotten about protection and how the stomach flu might have interfered with the pill. *Out of date condoms, too?* Her story sprang from a deeply rooted place in her heart, emotion visible in her watery eyes and flushed cheeks.

In the distance, I heard an engine starting, and I cocked my head toward the sound. "Are we alone now?"

Goldie nodded, and I took her with me, spreading out on the bed and pulling her into my arms. She snuggled against my chest, and the world had never felt more right.

"How many tests did you take?"

"You really know me well, don't you?" she said, circling her finger around the button of my polo shirt. "I took five…from five different brands."

I laughed over my surprise. "Doubt much?"

"Honestly, I couldn't help myself." She pushed up on her elbow to look me in the eye. "The pregnancy test aisle *slaps.* There're ones that give results in sixty seconds. Some use lines, and others spell it out for you.

In Spanish, too, which I thought was pretty cool." She smiled. "When all of them were positive, Prim got me in with her OB in Raleigh, and she said there's definitely a Baby Corda in the oven."

"I wish I'd been with you. If I wasn't such an ass, I would've been."

Goldie grabbed my hand and pressed it to her heart. "You were with me—with both of us—right here." She flashed me her genuine sunshine bright smile and gave me a wink. "Plus, there's always next time."

I grinned. "Damn straight. And a time after that?"

We fell into laughter, and I pulled her close to me. "When's our due date?"

"March twentieth."

I knew I was a creature of habit, and I bounced that date around in my head for a moment. As an engineer, I flourished in the world of proposals, designs, and deadlines. While I'd made providing for and protecting my family a priority, Goldie made intimacy natural and spontaneity a joy. I had about seven and a half months to prepare for drool and poopy diapers…and a calendar with sparkly markers to buy for our refrigerator door. "I can't wait to tell our families. Who else knows?"

"Mom, Prim, Billie, and Ace."

I sighed, picturing myself in her brother's shoes, and some guy coming to see me about Jess. *And her pregnant.*

"What is it?"

I shifted us onto our sides and caught her gaze. "I went to see your brother this morning to ask his permission to marry you. He was tough, but fair. I don't know how I'd have reacted in his shoes—like with Jess pregnant."

"You'd be fair, too. Especially if your sister told you she was in love." She lifted my hand and kissed my knuckles. "I told Ace everything right from the start."

"Christ, I can't imagine what your family thinks of me. I was such an ass."

She squeezed my arm. "No, you weren't. Besides, I'm pretty tough, and they knew I came home to work on the irrigation redesign—but also to figure things out. I was wanting to come home to you when I realized this," she said, pausing to rub her tummy, "this little peanut happened."

Peanut. I like it. I covered her hand, my smile stretching across my face. "You're *really* pregnant. I-I still can't believe it."

"Wait until you see me morning sick…or crying over burned toast. Then you'll believe it."

As Goldie fell into an easy dissertation about diet and exercise during pregnancy and her theory on natural childbirth, I listened, memorizing the bounce in her voice and animation of her expressions. When she reached for her knitting needles, showing me the rows of seafoam green yarn that would one day become a baby blanket, my heart stretched so thin I thought it might pop.

"Please, stop," I said, holding up my hand. "There's one thing we have to decide right here. Right now. When will you marry me? Wherever you want, however you want, but please…how soon?"

As Goldie bit her lower lip, looking all too sexy curled up with me on her bed, my phone rang. *James' ringtone.* After the fourth time, I glanced at Goldie, and she nodded. I pressed accept and hit the speaker button.

"Hey, little brother. I'm here with Gold—"

"Jesus, it's about time," James said with the bark of

a Rottweiler. "Don't you read your texts?"

I tapped the screen a couple times. "Sorry." I winked at Goldie. "We needed some privacy so—"

"Yeah, yeah, that's good, but I need you, Max. It's Anna. Her water broke, and we're at the hospital."

Goldie squealed, and I sat up. "We're on our way. Be there," I said, looking at her two fingers waving in the air, "in a couple hours."

"I'll be waiting for you," he said with a milder bark, adding, "And you, too, Goldie. We've missed you around here."

"Missed you all, too."

"We'll be on the road in ten minutes," I said, walking over to her half-packed suitcase.

"Yeah, drive safe…but get here fast, okay?"

With that, the call ended. I turned around in time for Goldie to spring into my arms. I hugged her, molding her body to mine.

A soft sigh lifted from her lips, and I knew I'd never grow tired of that sound…or any of her sounds. I adored her snuffling snore in heavy sleep, her off-pitch humming to songs on our playlist…her sensual moans when we made love. And I wanted to discover new sounds with her, like our child's palms slapping the water in the bathtub and lips slurping juice through a sippy cup.

During the weeks of separation from Goldie, I'd made peace with the fact my marriage was essentially an amicable cohabitation, efficient and economical. The divorce no longer registered as a failure in my mind. We'd had a partnership, and it simply ran its course.

Not once in nine years of marriage had the notion of two people becoming 'one' made sense to me. *But how could it when that requires vulnerability?*

I was in love with Goldie, and becoming one with her lived in every thought, decision, and hope in my heart. All the little things mattered, and I'd noticed them and missed them—had missed *her*—terribly when we were apart.

I reached for her hand, rubbing my thumb over the diamond ring on her finger. As our gazes met, I grinned at her like the lovestruck guy I was. "Would you like me to pull up the calendar on my phone?"

She inched closer, biting the corner of her mouth. "Impatient much…?"

Her tone, a sexy mix of gravelly and greedy, got a tug from my lips. I bent my knees to look straight into her eyes. "Absolutely. And just so you don't forget, I'm in love much, too." I leaned forward to kiss her, whispering, "You're my forever, Peach. My real-life truth and dare."

Epilogue

Ten Months Later
Sunday, May 8th 11:40 a.m.
Goldie

Our families gathered around us inside the chapel, bouquets of lilies, peonies, and baby's breath gracing the altar. A soft silence filled the air, and I gazed at my husband holding our child in his arms. The words had been spoken, the prayers recited, and now our boy was blessed in Baptism.

This ceremony punctuated what had been a year of firsts, beginning with my accepting a position at CDD, meeting Max and diving headfirst in love with him, and making this little guy, Daniel Gray Corda. Our joy pushed boundaries and was so much more precious for the fast yet winding road we took to get there. This year of firsts and dares and truths still overwhelmed me but my days of feeling less than enough were forgotten. *Love has a way of doing that to you.*

After the final Amen, Max met my gaze with a tenderness that made my heart thump wildly. He reached for my hand and cast me a secret smile. My breathing restored, I laced my fingers in his and leaned my head on his shoulder.

Afterward, we were off to a reception at the farm to celebrate both Daniel's baptism and Mother's Day. We had six mothers there from our family—my grandmother, both our moms, Annabel, Billie, and me—and dozens more counting our neighbors. Max and I stood side by side, our son sleeping in my arms, and greeted our friends.

Giggles and squeals came from the children swinging on swings in the backyard, and as Billie's two-year-old daughter zipped past us on her tricycle, little white basket filled with her stuffed animals, Max and I grinned at each other, mouthing the word, *peanuts.* Ever the protective guy, Max slowed her down long enough to ensure there'd be no repeat of sweet Charlie and the three foam pellets he'd stuffed in his ear last spring.

Ace and Thorne had filled the yard with refreshments and games—and a pig roasting on the family grill—all while doting on the various mothers with their trademark Vreeland charm. I quickly scanned the yard, spotting Jack, Leigh, and their children gathered near the pint-sized basketball goal. Sofia and her husband George relaxed on a pair of lawn chairs, sipping colorful drinks, though hers was alcohol-free. Their baby girl was due in September, and while Sofia had the nursery covered in a palette of pink, George had a red racer convertible set to go for his little speed princess.

My twin siblings, Sage and Billie, had set up one of our tents as a makeshift dressing room, complete with costumes and props, and Sage was presently playing narrator for a special rendition of "Goldenrod and the Three Bears." Max's mother took Daniel over to sit with my mom, and Max led us to a blanket beside James, Annabel, and their fast-crawling son, Michael.

As the children played their parts and the story

unfolded, I sensed something was missing. *Or someone.* My gaze flickered left and right, and I stole a peek over my shoulder.

Max leaned over and whispered in my ear. "I hear you thinking. Want me to help you find Prim?"

I smiled, continually amazed at his uncanny intuition, but shook my head. I stood up, blew him a kiss, and headed toward the house.

Once inside I heard the notes coming from the piano, and I followed the music straight to my sister. I scooted in next to Prim on the bench, laying my head on her shoulder while she sang and played a song by heart. When she finally lifted her fingers from the keys, she brought her hands to her lap.

"You finished your song," I said, beaming. "It's good. *Really* good."

"Glad you like it. It'll stay right here with the rest of them." Prim tapped her head, then glanced at her watch. "I'm sorry, but you know I've got to be at the hospital in a few hours, and it's a forty-five minute drive to Raleigh."

I nodded, hooking my arm in hers. "I'm so happy you could be here today. You were with me right from the start of this whole roller coaster."

"Yeah and look at you. Five pregnancy tests, one kick-ass Shembery Isle wedding, and eight hours of labor later, here you are. Daniel's amazing mother and having him baptized on Mother's Day."

"It'll happen for you, too. One day. Avery was just a jerk, okay? The right guy is—"

"Don't." Prim rose to her feet. "You know I hate being under the microscope. Drives me nuts." She stepped away from the piano, walked over to the sofa, and shrugged into her jacket. "You mind telling everyone bye for me?"

"Of course."

"I've got three nights on, so I probably won't see you guys before you leave."

I stood and walked over to my sister. "We'll be back in a month for the Fourth of July barbeque."

"So...I'll see you soon, yeah?"

I grabbed Prim in my arms, hugging her tight and whispering in her ear. "You know Billie's after me to get you to go out with the new biology teacher at the high school."

"Has she forgotten I don't live in Vista Falls?" She took a step backward. "Really, Billie needs to stick to sixth grade math and tell her husband to keep his assistant coach slash biology teacher on a short rope."

"Ouch," I said, crossing my arms.

"Sorry, but seriously...? I do go out on dates...as much as I can between hospital shifts." She lifted her chin. "I think you both need to remember I'm thirty, not fifty. Lots of women are still single at my age."

I gave her a nod. "I get it. But think about it, and in the meantime, I'll tell her to lay off, okay?"

"Thanks."

Prim paused at the mirror in the foyer, combing her long blond hair with her fingers. She had Mom's hair, straight and thick, and I watched as she pulled it into a sleek ponytail.

I stepped in behind her, dropping my chin on her shoulder, and she turned her head to kiss me on the cheek. "I love you, Goldie. Call me this week, okay?"

"I will. Love you, too," I said, my gaze following my sister out the door.

Like me, Prim didn't date in high school, and her college years also registered zero serious relationships. We'd often joked our lackluster love lives were due to our being two overly independent and highly intelligent, complex females. We liked to think we were in control of everything, but mostly we were in lockdown. *A little scared to trust someone with our hearts.*

I'd always thought this was ironic since Prim had the truest heart of all the Vreeland wildflowers, soaking up all of Mom's mushy English poems and sonnets. Prim loved to write in her journals, too. My lips stretched into a slow grin, recalling how when she was a girl, she used to dot the "i" in her name with a little heart and draw strings of them with a red pen across Mom's grocery lists. Once I found her journal lying on the piano bench and spotted a page with a giant heart on it, the words "C.B. caught me…and my heart." Granted, she was in middle school, and God knows those years were heavy on the mood swings, but to this day I don't know who C.B. was to my sister. *And probably never will.*

A little knot lodged in the back of my throat, and as if on cue—for whatever emotional moment I was having—my breasts began to tingle. I glanced at my watch and, guessing it was about time for Daniel's feeding, walked back outside.

I spotted Max, James, and Ace standing in a small circle, my big brother looking out of place with no baby in his arms. *His journalist girlfriend misses yet another family milestone…what a shocker.* How they still considered themselves a couple puzzled me.

Ace busied himself passing out fresh beer, pulling up short and waving a bottle at me. "There'll be none of this for you, newest mommy of the bunch."

"True," I said, taking Daniel from Max. "My little man doesn't want any of *that* messing with his supper."

Ace twisted his mouth and pulled on his beer, and Max laughed out loud. Moments later, Annabel joined James as he motorboated his son through the air. Max hooked his arm over my shoulder and led us inside to the kitchen.

I turned and kissed him, as fully as I could with Daniel in my arms. Max deepened the kiss, moving his lips over mine, sharing the air with me. He leaned back an inch, gazing at me with those gorgeous green eyes.

"You okay?"

I pressed a kiss to our baby's head, his dark hair soft against my lips. "Yeah."

"Prim's—"

"Gone. Evening shift." I shrugged my shoulder. "I told her we'd see her over the Fourth."

Max rubbed my arms with his hands. "We don't have to head back with the others tonight. We could stay this week if you'd like. There's nothing I can't do right here with Wi-Fi and Sofia a phone call away. Dad and James will cover anything else in the office." Our gazes locked. "I know that look, Peach. What d'you say we stay the week, then go home, and we'll come back for July Fourth," Max said, lifting Daniel in his arms.

A smile spread across my face because my husband knows me so well. I sat on the sofa, unbuttoning my blouse. "I'd love that. Thank you."

He eased in beside me. As I began nursing, he fixed his gaze on our son. "I love the little sounds he makes. He gets straight to the business of eating."

I tilted my head. "He definitely has his daddy's determination."

"I'm glad you pointed that out because," he said, brushing my cheek with the back of his hand, "something else I have is a plan involving you and me and a couple of nights alone." When my mouth dropped open, he leaned over Daniel's head and kissed my lips. "This is coming straight from your mom, and I quote, 'Seriously, Max? Get Goldie out of here. There's plenty of breastmilk in the freezer, and I want to take care of my grandson.' So, unless you want to buck your mom…?"

I listened as Max filled me in on the details about Ace asking us to christen his newest villa at the Old Rambler Bed and Breakfast. He leaned in closer, cupped his hand over Daniel's ear, and whispered wicked things about champagne, a whirlpool tub, and—

"Can we have a garden veggie pizza and cold beer?" I asked, not sure if my mouth watered over the idea of our favorite stay-in supper from Shembery Isle…or the promise of his mouth moving over every inch of my skin.

"Your wish is my command. So, is that a yes? After we close out this little celebration this afternoon, may I have you all to myself for a few days?" He nuzzled the soft spot behind my ear. "I want to go to that big oak tree by the creek and carve our initials in the trunk like your parents did."

My heart tightened in my chest. *Can he be more wonderful?* I gazed down at Daniel who'd fallen asleep at my breast, mouth open. My little man would be in excellent hands with my mother. *And I'll be in my favorite place…the very loving and skilled hands of my incredible husband.*

I peeked at Max from beneath my lashes, warmth radiating from deep in my heart, and reached out to touch that rogue curl over his brow. "Absolutely. I think your plan *slaps*."

A word about the author...

Ann enjoys spending time with family, trying out new recipes, and relaxing on her back porch to read and write. She's a member of Heart of Carolina Romance Writers, loves watching television dramas, and always has a great romance book in her hand. Connect with Ann at http://www.annmtrader.com.

Thank you for purchasing
this publication of The Wild Rose Press, Inc.

For questions or more information
contact us at
info@thewildrosepress.com.

The Wild Rose Press, Inc.
www.thewildrosepress.com